The Chronicles of Harriet Tubman: Freedonia

Balogun Ojetade

ISBN: 1481183508
ISBN-13: 978-1481183505

DEDICATION

For my mother, Almeater Swan, Harriet Tubman and "Stagecoach" Mary Fields, who taught me the true meaning of "Warrior Woman."

CONTENTS

ACKNOWLEDGMENTS

Since there is a trend among authors to thank famous people – some they met, some who transitioned long ago – shamelessly name-dropping to make them look bigger than perhaps they really are at the moment, I will jump on the bandwagon. After all, who am I to buck tradition? And who knows, perhaps – like those other authors who do this must – I will receive some benefit. So here goes. I wish to thank the following people: the Honorable Marcus Garvey and the Honorable Elijah Muhammad for promoting Black literacy; famed author and Poet Mari Evans, who held my son at dinner when he was a baby, as did Sonia Sanchez, who handed him to Mari Evans after he tried to bite Ms. Sanchez's nose; actor and martial arts master Ron Hall, who called me one day and said, "I like this Steamfunk Movement you've created and would like to work with you on a Steamfunk film project one day soon"; Harriet Tubman, who inspired me to write about Black heroes from history; Walter Mosley and Nnedi Okorafor, whose books are always before and after mine on bookshelves, and whose names always appear before and after mine in almanacs and many lists of Black writers – thanks for always being there, y'all; and last but not least, James Brown, the Godfather of Soul, whose daughter once helped me produce a film and who is a founding father of funk, which led to calling the Black / Afrikan expression of Steampunk Steam*funk*, which gave birth to this novel you now hold in your hands.

There are many more people I could thank, but I am much too modest to do so, thus I will stop here.

CHAPTER ONE

September 5, 1870

The tiny Mount Gilboa Chapel – Oella, Maryland's only church for its small, Black population – was an eye sore to the white mill workers who lived nearby. They dared not touch the 28 feet by 42 feet structure of ashlar and rubble, however because something dark and powerful protected this place. And it wasn't Baby Jesus or the Heavenly Hosts.

The millworkers did not know what dark forces haunted that church, but the few men who ventured to burn it down all met terrible fates. One among the unfortunate, a rotund fellow with the surname of Snodgrass, was found on the road outside the church with the heel of his left foot stuffed into his mouth and his navel pressed against his buttocks. After the Snodgrass incident, the millworkers decided it would be best to leave Mount Gilboa in peace.

Although the populace of Oella – even the members of the church – believed Mount Gilboa Chapel to be haunted, something more frightening than any ghost lived twenty feet below its flooring. In a secret sub-basement lived the Alchemist; Professor Amschel Kleinhopper; Benjamin Banneker.

One of Banneker's human-sized knolls – his sentient constructs of grass, soil, stone and clockwork – pushed its master's gurney into a nearly upright position.

Banneker stared at the doorway before him. The plague doctor's mask that he was cursed to wear for all eternity concealed the sardonic smile stretched across his face.

A tall, lanky white man crept into the room. The man was well tanned, with leathery skin. His wrinkled face was nearly buried under a thick, grey beard.

"John Brown," Banneker crooned. "I am honored by your intrusion. What brings you to fair Oella?"

"We need your help and are prepared to pay you handsomely for it," John Brown replied.

Banneker tilted his head. "We? That fetid

aroma, underneath the Florida water you wear in an attempt to cover it, must belong to whomever – or whatever – accompanies you."

"Hey," a muffled voice came from beneath John Brown's shirt, vest and town-coat. "I *can* hear you."

"Interesting." Banneker nodded toward Brown's chest. "Show me."

John Brown unbuttoned his vest and the cotton shirt underneath. Caleb Butler – the cowboy King of the Ghuls – batted his eyes, which were irritated by the dozens of candles that illuminated Banneker's office.

Caleb smiled. "Mr. Banneker, I've heard so much about you."

Banneker's voice was warm and congenial. "Good things, I hope."

"As good as they *can* be, for a nig..." The words seemed to die upon Caleb's lips. "For a man of your...persuasion."

"I *can* be quite persuading when I need to be," Banneker replied. "How about you?"

"I pray we can persuade you to help us out," Brown said. "As you can see, we are in quite dire straits. We are sure you can help us out, though."

“You want to separate from each other.” Banneker said.

“Yes, sir,” Caleb replied. “We’ve been closer than flies and cow patties for five years, which was fine at first, ‘cause we thought it’d make it easier to kill that old witch Harriet Tubman and her compadres, but they went into hidin’ after Stagecoach Mary and that old Giantess, Mama Maybelle damn near killed each other.”

“I can certainly help out,” Banneker said. “But, as you said, it will cost you handsomely.”

“Name your price!” Caleb replied.

“I want you to kill Baas Bello,” Banneker said.

“Hell, that’d be our pleasure!” Caleb said.

“Thank you, for making this easy on us, Dr. Banneker,” John Brown said. “We intended to kill Baas Bello for aiding General Moses, anyway.”

“Killing Baas Bello by conventional means is no simple task,” Banneker replied. “His infernal gadgets are unmatched and, as you already know, he is protected by Harriet Tubman and Stagecoach Mary. That is quite a formidable trio.”

"What do you suggest, then?" John Brown asked.

"I suggest killing Baas Bello," Banneker answered. "But not the Baas Bello of *this* reality."

Caleb snickered. "You talk like there is some other reality. This some of that jungle mumbo-jumbo?"

Banneker tapped the plush leather padding of his gurney three times with the back of his head. A low hiss escaped the back of it, accompanied by a blast of steam, which shot toward the ceiling. The gurney rolled forward a few feet, stopping inches from Brown and Caleb. "Hundreds of years ago, Baas Bello became aware of the existence of another universe; one identical to ours in every way. Each of us has a double there. Baas was somehow linked to his. They were fully aware of the existence and goings on of each other."

"Baas is the only one with such a link?" Brown inquired.

"Apparently, we and our doubles are merely reflections of the same spirit in different realities," Banneker replied. "Thus, when our double dies, we die also. Baas is the only one known to share the same thoughts and feelings with his double, however."

"And how do you know all this?" Caleb asked.

"Baas confided this to Marie Laveau when they were married," Banneker replied. "Shortly before Madame Laveau's last encounter with Baas – one you rudely interrupted, from what I am told – she revealed these amazing truths to me, in hopes it would help me kill the old bastard in case he did not comply with her demands."

"But isn't Baas Bello protected by Moses and Black Mary in that reality, too?" Brown asked.

"I do not know," Banneker answered. "However, I *do* know that the people in that reality do not possess the gifts that we do. Except for Baas Bello, that is."

"So what...we just gon' leave this reality and fly on off to another one?" Caleb said. "That'd be one hell of a dirigible, wouldn't it?"

Caleb and John Brown laughed. Banneker was silent.

Banneker cleared his throat. When the laughter subsided, he spoke again.

"Baas created what he calls the Spirit-Engine. It tears a chasm in this reality that leads into the next."

"And where is this Spirit-Engine?" John Brown asked.

"The Whitechapel District of London, England," Banneker replied. "My ship – *Kraken's Almanac* – will get you to London posthaste. The rest will be up to you. Once I have proof my old master is dead, I will grant you what you wish."

"Agreed," Brown said with a nod.

"Always wanted to see England," Caleb said. "I hear those British girls got good..."

"I will have my carriage take you to *Kraken's Almanac*," Banneker said, interrupting Caleb. "The crew will be prepared and ready to set sail."

CHAPTER TWO

"I suggest killing Baas Bello, but not the Baas Bello of this *reality."*

The words echoed in Mary Elizabeth Bowser's ears. In fact, the entire conversation between her employer and the man – or was it two men – who visited him played back in her mind's ear, over and over. She recalled every word, just as she did with everything else she heard or witnessed. It was a gift she possessed all her life; a gift that made her the perfect spy.

After the war, the Union had no more use for the Black Dispatches. In fact, most were feared because of their skills and their gifts and virtually unknown outside of their covers. Only Harriet Tubman had gone on to find success.

Monsters would always need to be hunted. Thankfully, she had stayed in contact with the old soldier, for it was Harriet who introduced Mary Elizabeth to Baas Bello and it was Baas who hired her to keep a close eye on Benjamin Banneker.

She had taken on the cover of Betty Brown, a mentally challenged, but very skilled and experienced housekeeper. Banneker "caught" her stealing food from his steamboat one night. She was almost killed by a patrolling knoll, but Banneker stopped the creature and spared Mary Elizabeth's life. He looked into poor Betty Brown's background and found she had skill in the domestic arts, but could barely find work because of her mental deficiencies. Banneker took her in. She was the perfect employee for him – capable of caring for his lair and his Steamboat, but not enough sense to articulate what she witnessed to others or to report his murders and other crimes to the authorities.

Mary Elizabeth rapped on Banneker's office door with her tiny brown fist.

"Come in," a voice on the other side of the door called.

Mary lumbered into the office, flashing a crooked smile at Banneker, who lay nearly upright on the gurney he was always strapped to. "Mo'nin', Missuh Banka! How you be?"

"I'm just fine, Betty," Benjamin Banneker replied. "How can I help you?"

"I-I jus' got dis letta from de man," Mary Elizabeth replied, holding a piece of paper above her bowed head. "He wouldn't read it to me, do'."

"Do you want me to read it?" Banneker asked. His voice was always kind with poor Betty.

"If you'd be so kind, suh," Mary Elizabeth said. "I-I knows you a busy man..."

"Nonsense," Banneker replied. "I always have time for you, Betty. Bring it closer, so I can see."

Mary Elizabeth walked toward Banneker's gurney, holding the letter at the level of his eyes.

She could see his eyes under his mask. They flitted back and forth as he perused the letter's words. "It's from your brother, Elijah. It says your mother has fallen very ill and that they need you to make some concoction for her breathing."

"I makes a tonic for her lungs, jus' like my granny taught me," Mary Elizabeth said. "Ol' Betty ain't as dumb as folks say."

"That's right, Betty," Banneker crooned. "I believe one day, you will prove to be smarter than I."

Mary Elizabeth blushed. "Aw, now, Missuh Banka, don't be funnyin' me!"

A whistling chuckle slithered from under Banneker's mask. "I tell you what, Betty...go back to Chicago for a few days. Attend to your mother and then come back after she's back on her feet."

"Oh, no suh, Missuh Banka," Mary Elizabeth gasped. "I couldn't do dat! I gots to tend to you!"

"The knolls will take care of me until you return," Banneker replied. "I insist. In fact, I'll pay for your trip there and back and throw in a few hundred dollars to ensure your comfort while you are away."

"Thank you, suh!" Mary Elizabeth squealed. "Thank you!"

"Thank me by coming back and telling me your mother is once again doing well," Banneker said.

"I will, suh," Mary Elizabeth said. "I'm gon' go pack, now. God bless you!"

"Betty,,,"

Mary Elizabeth could hear the disappointment in his voice. “Suh?”

“What did I say about God?”

“De only *real* ‘God’ is de scientis’.”

“Right!” Banneker replied. “And the only true religion?”

“Science,” Mary Elizabeth said, staring at the floor.

“Very good!” Banneker said. “If I could move my hands, I would applaud you.”

“I believe one day you will be able to,” Mary Elizabeth said, mimicking Banneker’s voice. “An’ I ain’t funnyin’ you, neither!”

The room was filled with Banneker’s whistling, wheezing laughter.

Mary Elizabeth laughed with him, but could not wait until she was finally out of his presence and on her way to Chicago to report to Baas Bello.

CHAPTER THREE

September 7, 1870

A pair of large dice, carved from a bear's femur and covered by its fur, danced erratically against the brass handlebars of the monowheel as Harriet Tubman peeled out of the driveway leading from Trail's End – the stately mansion of George Lemuel Woods, Governor of Oregon – onto Lincoln Street.

Harriet flexed her right wrist backward, revving the monowheel's engine. She released the clutch, which was built into the left handlebar and shifted the monowheel into fourth gear with her left foot.

The engine hissed; the stack that protruded from it belched a cloud of steam and then the monowheel jetted forward.

Cold wind smacked Harriet's body, pinning her soft, blue cotton dress to her short, sinewy frame. The large, triangular lapels of her leather jacket fluttered against Harriet's smooth, hazelnut-toned face.

She zipped through the bustling neighborhood in the heart of Salem, quickly closing upon a towering, brass skeleton clock that loomed in the distance.

The aether torch at the apex of the clock – affectionately called 'Shiny Bones' by the residents of Salem – glowed with an intense, white light.

Shiny Bones also served as the lighthouse for the airships that patrolled the skies over Oregon.

Harriet darted into the Constabulary's parking lot, speeding past the fleet of steam-powered, horseless carriages into the section marked 'Gatekeepers'.

She slid into her parking space – lot number 010 – and then leapt from her seat. Her shoes struck the pavement with a dull thud.

"Hey, Gatekeeper...how are you this fine morning?"

Harriet turned toward the source of the

rich tenor voice. "Constable Kojoe! I told you, I ain't no Gatekeeper; I'm just here for a short spell, until I help get yo' problem with them Rogues fixed once and for all. But anyhow, how *you* be?"

Constable Kojoe's lips curled upward into a broad grin. His brilliant, white teeth were in stark contrast to his nearly black skin. "I'm better, now that I'm laying eyes upon you."

Harriet rolled her eyes and shook her head. "You better keep yo' eyes on Liu Fong, there."

The shackled giant standing at Constable Kojoe's left flank leered at Harriet. "No worries, Gatekeeper; I'm a kinder...gentler man, now that I'm married and all."

"You just broke your father-in-law's jaw, four ribs and his right femur," Constable Kojoe said, yanking on the iron cuffs about Liu Fong's wrists.

"I didn't kill him," Liu Fong replied. "But I *will* kill you, if you yank on those cuffs again."

"I am *so* afraid," Constable Kojoe snickered, yanking the cuffs a bit harder.

Liu Fong snarled and clinched his fists. His massive forearms flexed, expanding his thick wrists. The handcuffs snapped open and fell to the ground.

The giant hammered his elbow into the back of the constable's head.

Constable Kojoe collapsed to the ground.

Liu Fong turned and darted across the parking lot.

Harriet gave chase.

She exploded upward, pouncing onto Liu Fong's massive back.

The giant tried to shake her loose, but Harriet already had her arms wrapped around his neck and her legs clamped about his waist, holding him in a boa constrictor-like grip.

Harriet squeezed hard with her arms, compressing Liu Fong's neck to half its girth.

The giant's scowling face went slack and then he collapsed to his knees.

Harriet released his neck and the giant fell, face down, onto the pavement.

"Sleep tight," Harriet said, patting Liu Fong on the top of his bald head.

She then sprinted over to Constable Kojoe, who pulled himself to his knees as he gently massaged the lump on the back of his head.

"Did you get him?" Constable Kojoe asked.

"He's out like a baby after breastfeedin'." Harriet replied.

Harriet helped the constable to his feet. "Better go get him before he wakes up."

Constable Kojoe sprinted toward the unconscious giant. He paused for a second and called out to Harriet. "Let me repay you for this...how about dinner...tonight?"

Harriet laughed. "Son, you can't handle this. Besides, I'm old enough to be yo' mama."

"Maybe that's what I find so intriguing about you," the constable replied.

"Lawd!" Harriet shook her head, turned on her heels and then stepped through the Constabulary Station's brass double doors.

Harriet sauntered toward the lift. She reached into the breast pocket of her jacket and withdrew a copper key. She slipped the key into a hole in the lift's door and turned it counter clockwise.

The door slid open.

Harriet hopped into the lift. The door slid

shut behind her. She slipped the key into the hole on the interior side of the door and turned the key clockwise. A hissing sound followed and the lift began to rise, coming to a halt a minute later. The door slid open and Harriet stepped off and into a long corridor. Facing her was a door marked 'Chief Constable'. Harriet pushed the door open and stepped inside of the capacious office.

Chief Constable Magaska Hota sat before her. Sweat rolled down the furrows in his forehead and his reddish-brown skin had gone a bit pale.

Harriet raised her right fingertips to the corner of her brow in salute.

The Chief Constable returned the salute and then pointed toward a chair that sat in front of his desk. "Take a seat, Harriet."

Harriet lowered herself into the chair. "I got your message, Chief Constable. Is there a breach of The Gate?"

"We don't know," the Chief Constable sighed. "But Shi Yan Bo was found dead this morning."

Harriet sat bolt upright, as if someone had struck her. "What? Since you called me in on this, it must be murder and the Governor Woods must think it's related to the Green Lands."

"He was most definitely murdered," Chief Constable Magaska Hota replied. "And the Council wants to cover all the bases. I mean, damn...a monk...the father of Aether Tech...murdered? Wakantanka, help us all...Kun-Lun District is going to be up in arms."

"When do you want me to go to Kun-Lun?"

"Yesterday," the Chief replied.

Harriet rose from her seat. "I'm on it, Chief!"

She pushed the door open and prepared to leave. "Gotta pick up a few things from my locker first."

"And, Harriet," The Chief Constable called.

"Yeah, Chief?" Harriet said, peering over her shoulder.

"Try not to kill too many people or blow up too much stuff on this one."

"You're asking a lot, Chief," Harriet replied. "But, I'll try."

She flashed the Chief a brilliant smile, waved and stepped into the lobby. Harriet turned to her left; just past the Chief Constable's office was another door. She withdrew a small, silver key from her breast pocket and used it to unlock the door. She opened it and stepped into a room illuminated by aether light.

The walls of the room were lined with large, bronze lockers, each six feet in height and four feet wide. On the face of each locker was a brass plate with six tiny, bronze levers protruding from it. Using the tip of her well-manicured index finger, Harriet pushed the first lever to her left down; she pushed the second one up; the third up; and so on, until she had completed the combination.

A whirring noise came from inside the locker and then the door opened a crack.

Harriet pushed the door open and stepped inside the locker. The door shut behind her and she found herself in a pristine white room that seemed to run on forever. Before her were endless rows of weapons, armor and strange looking devices.

"Corset...shotgun...engram iconoscope," she shouted.

A few minutes later, something in the distance sped toward her. As the speeding object drew close, a shiny, silver table came into view. Atop the table was a silver cage and inside the cage were a few items.

The table came to a smooth stop a yard from Harriet. Harriet approached the table and inspected the items in the cage. Satisfied, she removed them and the table sped off, disappearing into the alabaster distance.

Harriet wrapped the crimson, leather corset around her torso. The corset tightened around her body and then molded itself to fit her frame. This marvel of technology had protected her from many a bullet, claw and stinger.

She picked up the shotgun and admired it. The weapon – customized to her specifications – was as beautiful as it was deadly…like Harriet, which is why she named it "Junior". The steam-powered, semi-automatic weapon was a masterwork of iron, bronze and brass – Baas Bello's best weapon, yet. She slipped a bronze ammunition drum into the weapon and then slapped it to lock it into place.

Harriet then picked up a copper box by its handle and walked toward the exit. The door flung open. She stepped out of the locker and the door slammed shut behind her.

Harriet exited the locker room and walked back to the lift. After entering it, she slipped her key into the door and turned it clockwise.

The lift rose higher. When it stopped, Harriet removed her key and the door slid open.

Harriet stepped out onto the roof, where two dirigibles sat. One, with 'Constabulary' – in brass plating – embossed on the mahogany frame of its carriage; the other, smaller dirigible, with 'Gatekeeper One' engraved into its bronze-framed carriage.

Sitting in a booth near the airships were a woman and two men. Their crisp, indigo uniforms and the trio of gold stripes on their sleeve cuffs informed their positions as airship pilots.

One of the men approached Harriet, raising his hand in salute. "Good afternoon, Gatekeeper Tubman."

"I keep tellin' y'all, I ain't no Gatekeeper," Harriet replied. "I'm only here as a favor to Baas Bello...and 'cause the pay is good. Anyhow, I need to take the Bird up...heading to Kun-Lun."

"I can take you, but I don't speak Mandarin and Constable Yip is off today." The pilot said.

"I speak enough Mandarin for the both of us, child," Harriet replied. "Now, let's get movin'."

"I'm Constable Haokah," the pilot said as he unlocked the door to the airship's carriage.

"Wiyuskingyang wangchingyangke le," Harriet said – *"Pleased to meet you!"*

"Your Lakota is excellent!" Constable Haokah said.

"Lila pilamalaye," Harriet replied – *"Thank you, very much."*

Harriet hopped up into the airship. Constable Haokah followed her, locking the door behind him.

"Have a seat and we'll be on our way," the pilot said.

Harriet placed her weapon and the engram iconoscope on a mahogany bench and then plopped down on the bench in front of it. The oxblood leather felt cool, soft and relaxing. She leaned back, resting her head on the plush cushion and slipped into sleep as the airship took to the skies.

****

"We will arrive in Kun-Lun in ten minutes, Gatekeeper...umm. Miss Tubman," Constable Haokah shouted over the roar of the steam engine.

Harriet stretched and then moved to the bench behind her to retrieve her belongings.

"I will be landing atop the Kun-Lun District constabulary station," the constable said. "From there, a rickshaw will take you to the crime scene. It will also bring you back when you're done."

"Thank you," Harriet replied with a nod.

She peeked out of the portcullis and admired the view. Kun-Lun was a marvel of grand architecture. Residential towers, pagodas and watchtowers of crimson brick and black tiled roofs dotted the district. The imposing Elder House – the complex in which the two Elders from Kun-Lun, and their families, resided – sported roofs constructed of yellow tiles. Kun-Lun was a place of great beauty and many secrets.

While the residents of Kun-Lun, of which ninety-nine percent of them were Chinese, were loyal to Oregon – after all, the unified African contingent, led by Baas Bello, that purchased the African slaves out of bondage in South America had also purchased the freedom of the Chinese from indentured servitude – they were still very close-knit and tight-lipped about the goings on in Kun-Lun.

Constable Haokah landed the dirigible upon the roof of the constabulary station. He then walked to the door and slid it open. "See you soon," he said, giving Harriet a crisp salute.

Harriet returned the salute. "See you in a couple of hours, child."

She exited the airship and ran toward the elevator.

She took the elevator down to street level and then exited the constabulary station into its parking lot, where a rickshaw awaited her.

"Afternoon, Gatekeeper," the rickshaw driver said, tilting his top-hat. His long, black hair fell over his youthful face.

"Wuan, child," Harriet replied, stepping up into the single passenger, cycle rickshaw. "Ni hao ma?" – *"Good afternoon, child. How are you?"*

"Wo hen hao, ni ne?" – *"I am fine, and you?"* The teenager replied.

"Wo hen hao, xie xie," Harriet said – *"I am fine, thank you."*

The rickshaw driver's powerful legs moved like pistons on the pedals of the rickshaw's front wheel and the rickshaw went sailing through traffic, passing other rickshaws, penny-farthings and the occasional horse-drawn carriage on the road.

A half hour later, the rickshaw passed through the red, wooden gates of the Lan Su Garden.

Harriet had visited this beautiful garden many times, but never on such terrible terms.

She had even shared tea at the Penjing exhibit with Shi Yan Bo once, when Baas Bello took her along on one of his many meetings with the monk. The encounter was peaceful...serene. And now, very surreal, for Shi Yan Bo was now dead in nearly the same spot where they shared Long Jing tea.

The rickshaw driver stopped at the Penjing exhibit. "The world landscape in miniature", Shi Yan Bo called it. And so it was – rocks, moss, plants, small figurines made of mud, boats, tiny rivers and miniscule buildings or a tiny forest – all in one clay pot.

Lying face down among the tiny trees was Shi Yan Bo. His yellow, cotton robe was torn on the right side. Harriet inspected the area closer and found a large, black bruise on the monk's right side. She pressed her fingers on the spot and the bruise sank in about an inch.

"Broken ribs," someone said from behind her. *"Four of them."*

Harriet peered over her shoulder. Standing

behind her was a tall woman, dressed in a silk, royal blue tunic and matching trousers. Her skin was smooth and well-tanned and her straight, black hair was pulled back and braided in a single ponytail that fell to the middle of her back. A light breeze blew the woman's clothes against her body, revealing a well-toned form.

"You're a Gatekeeper," Harriet said.

"Yes," the woman replied. "My name is Pei-Pei Ming."

"You're new," Harriet said. "I'm Harriet Tubman."

"I know," Pei said. "Your exploits are quite...celebrated."

"Welcome aboard, Gatekeeper," Harriet said, standing and giving Pei a warm hug. "Hell of a first case you got, child."

"Indeed," Pei said nodding.

"Any witnesses?"

"Four," Pei answered. "I took the liberty of escorting them all to the teahouse."

"Good work," Harriet said, slipping her shotgun into the sheath on her back with one hand, while grabbing the engram iconoscope with the other. "Lead the way!"

Harriet followed Pei a short distance along a road that led to a stone bridge, which arched over a large pond filled with coy.

The two women crossed the bridge. The spicy-sweet aroma of tea licked at Harriet's nostrils.

The teahouse – an edifice constructed of black brick, with a roof of red tile – stood just before them. Harriet sauntered inside, five people sat, sipping tea and chatting quietly.

Upon spotting Harriet, the teahouse fell silent.

"Ni hao," Harriet said, in greeting, to the quintet of teahouse patrons.

They returned the greeting – "Ni hao." – *"Hello."*

"I am Harriet Tubman," Harriet said, continuing to speak to them in Mandarin Chinese. "I knew Master Bo; my friend and teacher – Baas Bello – and Master Bo was friends. We done all suffered a great loss today and I will do my best to find the person who did this and bring them to justice."

"We already know who did it," an elderly man spat. "One of your 'blood brothers'.

"You're saying the perpetrator was a

Negro?"

"Of course," the man replied. "Who, but a Negro would dress so...ridiculously gaudy?"

The other witnesses nodded in agreement.

Harriet closed her eyes and took in a deep breath. She concentrated on the beating of her heart – as Baas had taught her years ago – and slowed it down, calming herself. "I know y'all upset right now, but please, do not turn this into a racial issue. The Negro, Chinese and Indian done worked together for over twenty years here in Oregon and is now the wealthiest and most technologically advanced state in this country because of that unity."

The faces of the witnesses shifted from scowls to masks of frustration and sorrow.

Harriet sat the engram iconoscope on a table and then pressed a small button in its handle. The device opened to reveal what looked like a large crystal ball with five silver nodes dotting its surface; on one side of this "ball", protruded a crystal rod. At the end of the rod were four needles. Harriet removed four small canvas bags – each containing another set of needles – and handed them to Pei.

"This is an engram iconoscope," Harriet explained to the witnesses. "It records memories.

Most people do not consciously recall all that they see, but the engram iconoscope will. All you gots to do is think about the event; concentrate on it; the iconoscope will do the rest."

Harriet pointed toward the needles at the tip of the rod. "I am gonna insert these needles into acupuncture points at the base of your neck and it will record exactly what you saw. Most of y'all are familiar with acupuncture, so you know this procedure will be painless. Do y'all have any questions?"

"Can *she* do it?" A woman asked, nodding toward Gatekeeper Pei-Pei Ming.

"I *can,*" Pei replied. "However, Miss Tubman has much more experience with such things. Respect her, please."

"No, it's fine," Harriet said, handing the engram iconoscope to Pei. "I want you all to be comfortable."

Pei nodded and then handed the packs of needles to Harriet. Pei then stepped behind the woman who requested that she do the procedure and slowly inserted the needles into the base of her neck.

Images swirled within the engram iconoscope's ball, bonding to the aether within it. Slowly, the images steadied and grew clear.

Shi Yan Bo knelt before a miniature tree, pruning it. From the angle, it was obvious the woman stood on the bridge watching the monk.

A moment later, a person seemed to fall from the sky, landing a yard or so from Master Bo. The person appeared to be a male approximately six feet tall and weighing between one hundred-eighty and two hundred pounds. He was dressed in a candy apple red, wool suit, red gloves and red leather boots. A huge brimmed, red boss-of-the-plains hat – with a peacock feather protruding from it – concealed his face.

Startled, the monk leapt to his feet.

The man in the red suit exploded forward, whipping his rear leg in a wide arc toward the monk's torso.

The man's shin slammed into Shi Yan Bo's ribcage. The monk's robes shredded from the sheer power of the blow and he was sent tumbling sideways across the road.

The old monk struggled to his feet as the man-in-the-red-suit sauntered toward him.

Shi Yan Bo limped toward the bridge.

His assailant leapt toward him, reaching out toward the monk with outstretched fingers.

The man-in-the-red-suit thrust the fingers of one hand into Shi Yan Bo's neck as his other hand grabbed a fistful of the monk's long, white hair.

The man shoved Shi Yan Bo's head forward as he pulled the fingers buried in the monk's neck toward the old man's spine.

A torrent of blood erupted from the four deep gashes in Shi Yan Bo's neck.

The monk stumbled forward a few feet and then collapsed onto his face. He shuddered once and then lay still.

The man-in-the-red-suit turned away from Shi Yan Bo's lifeless body and calmly walked off, eventually disappearing among the fir trees.

Each witness' memory showed the same scene, but from different angles. However, none of them could see the killer's face, so his identity – and ethnicity – remained a mystery.

"Thank you all," Harriet said, packing up the engram iconoscope. "Gatekeeper Ming will stay here with you until the constabulary arrives.

"Actually, I am going with you," Pei Ming said. "Orders from both of our Chief Constables; I received them while you were en route here.

"Two of us working a murder?" Harriet said, shaking her head."The Governor obviously want this case closed quick!"

"It appears so," Pei replied.

"Once this gets out to the public, things between Kun-Lun and Songhai could get ugly," Harriet said. "Let's go!"

Harriet and Pei exited the teahouse. Harriet placed her hand on Pei Ming's shoulder. "Wait; we have to call you some transport; I'm in a single passenger rickshaw."

"No problem," Pei Ming said. "Upon initiation, the Masters gifted me with a subdermal temporal-spatial displacement engine."

"Moving sideways through time, huh?"Harriet said. "Thought that was just a theory. You Chinese are making advances that would even impress Baas."

"You would be astounded," Pei said. "We have even learned to eat with spoons and forks!"

"Funny," Harriet said, rolling her eyes. "Meet me on the roof of the constabulary station in forty-five minutes."

A luminous, purple gash in the air appeared before Gatekeeper Ming. She thrust her right leg into the tear in the world. "I'll be there in twenty."

Pei stepped sideways into the gash, disappearing from view as it closed.

"Lawd…I gotta get me one of those things!" Harriet said, shaking her head.

She sprinted to the rickshaw.

"Let's go," Harriet said, leaping into her seat. "Get me to the station in less than twenty minutes and I'll give you a tip of two silver coins!"

"What?!" The rickshaw driver gasped. "Two silver coins? Let's go!"

The rickshaw driver pedaled harder than he had ever done before. The rickshaw sped out of the garden and hit the street.

"Lawd, child!" Harriet said." Keep up this pace and I just might double that tip!"

****

"Another one?" Harriet sighed.

"Yes and this one is a child," Chief Constable Magaska Hota replied.

"Lawd!" Harriet gasped. "Where?"

“This is where it gets really bad,” the Chief Constable replied. “Her body was found in the stacks at the Willamette University Library. Witnesses say the murderer was Chinese.”

“We need to get there before the students start protesting and the press gets wind of this,” Pei-Pei Ming said.

“Too late,” the Chief replied. “The students started protesting about an hour ago. Several Chinese students have been attacked, as has a Dr. Doc-Fai Hung – a professor in the Chinese studies department. We have a squad of constables there keeping the situation under control, but I need you to take care of this...and fast!”

Harriet and Pei Ming saluted the Chief Constable and headed out the door of his office.

“We’re on it, Chief Constable,” Harriet said as she dashed out of the room. Pei-Pei Ming followed closely behind her.

“It’s rush hour, so we’ll take the airship again,” Harriet said. “Unless you wanna poof us over there with your displacement engine.”

“I can only transport myself,” Pei Ming said. “Myself, plus up to fifty pounds.”

“The airship it is then,” Harriet said. Let’s

go, Gatekeeper."

****

The dirigible landed on the grass-covered courtyard, which the schools and dormitories of Willamette University encircled.

Harriet leapt out of the dirigible. Pei-Pei Ming followed her.

A ring of constables pushed back a seething mass of students who shouted demands of justice.

Harriet and Pei pushed their way through the crowd. Recognizing Harriet, the constables parted for a moment to let them into the cordoned area outside of the library, where the girl's body lay.

Inside the library, at the top level of the stacks, Constable Kojoe stood beside the corpse. He smiled upon seeing Harriet. "Greetings and salutations, Gatekeeper Tubman!"

Harriet rolled her eyes. "Constable Kojoe, this is my partner, Pee-pee Ming...Pee-pee, this is Constable Kojoe."

"Pee-pee?" Constable Kojoe whispered.

"It's Pei-Pei – *pay*...pay – not Pee-pee," Pei Ming said, shaking her head. "Touché, partner."

Harriet flashed Pei-Pei a sly smile as she knelt down beside the corpse, which – like Shi Yan Bo – lay face down.

“Who is she?” Harriet asked, as she inspected the girl’s mahogany face.

“Amut Sut Hotep,” Constable Kojoe said. “Sixteen years old; second year, pre-med major; straight A-student and Secretary of the Student Union.”

Amut Sut Hotep’s silk, turquoise blouse had been nearly completely torn from her body. Deep cuts were on her right forearm and her right baby finger was severed at the second joint. Carved deep into the girl’s back were three Chinese characters.

“War,” Pei-Pei Ming said, reading the blood-encrusted wounds.

“How many witnesses?” Harriet asked.

“Three,” Constable Kojoe replied. “They’re in a meeting room downstairs.”

“Let’s get this over with, then,” Harriet sighed.

Like the witnesses to the murder of Shi Yan Bo, the witnesses to Amut Sut Hotep’s tragic death were interfaced with the engram iconoscope. In the witnesses’ memories of the murder, Amut was reading the ancient Zulu epic, *Indaba* – a favored classic among the Black populace of Oregon – when a man in a red, traditional, silk Chinese tunic and trousers and red silk gloves ascended the ladder that led up to the stacks. The man's face was concealed by a crimson mask formed in the image of a demon with bulging, yellow eyes, ears the size of bird wings and wicked-looking fangs protruding from a snarling, twisted maw.

Spotting the man in the mask, Amut sprang to her feet and attempted to kick the man off the ladder, but he was too quick for her and leapt to the platform of the stack, landing beside her.

Amut backpedaled away from the man. He closed on her, slashing at her neck with what appeared to be a jade-handled straight razor. The student threw up her arms to shield against the deadly strikes. She winced as – several times – her skin opened to reveal the flesh underneath. Blood sprayed with each wound, leaving a red mist in the air.

The man in the mask slammed his shoulder into Amut's solar plexus and she collapsed to her knees as the air rushed from her lungs.

The man wrapped his fingers around

Amut's neck and then slammed her face into the floor. Blood trickled from her mouth as a tooth rolled from between her lips and bounced along the floor of the stack.

The man in the mask then mounted Amut's back, straddling her waist with his knees and cut away her blouse with his weapon. He then proceeded to carve into her back with the razor.

Amut screamed as he mercilessly ripped at her young flesh with the razor. After a minute of agony, the girl fell still.

The man in the mask rose to his feet, looked around at the witnesses, waved to them and then descended the ladder. He sauntered toward the rear exit and a moment later he was gone.

With the information gathered from the witnesses, Harriet and Pei-Pei left the library as Constable Kojoe gathered written statements.

"Thoughts?" Harriet asked.

"I think we have definite Green activity," Pei-Pei replied. "Possibly a Skin-Walker; maybe even a Wendigo."

"A Skin-Walker? Maybe," Harriet said. "A Wendigo? No. A Wendigo would have eaten them before their hearts stopped beating...they can't help themselves. It might not be a Green at all, though. The last breach of the Gate was six months ago; it was a Night Howler and *I* put *that* one down."

Pei nodded.

"One thing I *do* know is that whoever – or whatever – is doin' these killins wants to set off a war between the Chinese and Negro communities," Harriet said.

"Who stands to gain from such a war?" Pei asked.

"Two groups," Harriet answered. "The Greens...and the First Nation community"

"The First Nation? Their War Chief...Wabli Ska?" Pei Ming said. "You think he is behind this?"

"He's the most vocal – and the most popular – separatist in Oregon," Harriet said. "He believes the First Nation would have overcome the Europeans eventually, but when the Negro and Chinese forefathers built Oregon, they pushed the Europeans to retaliate by awakening the Old Ones from their thousand year slumber, which forced the First Nations to flee into Oregon in order to escape the Greens that invaded their lands."

"He was once a constable was he not?" Pei asked.

"So they say," Harriet replied. "He is the older brother of Baas' son-in-law, Talltrees and a close friend. That was a long time ago, though."

"So, when do we bring him in for questioning?"

"We don't," Harriet answered. "Wabli Ska is the Chief Constable's son...we don't want to cause the Chief Constable unnecessary grief on a hunch. We're going to Tipi Wowahwa District and interrogating him there."

"Now?"

"No, child; I promised to meet Black Mary for dinner," Harriet replied. "We'll meet up after."

More students gathered on the yard, their faces masks of sorrow and fury. Several of them pointed toward Harriet and Pei-Pei.

"Better use that displacement engine," Harriet said. "Those students ain't taking too kindly to Chinese faces right now."

"Alright," Pei-Pei said, stepping into the tear in the world that had already formed. "I'll see you onboard the airship."

Pei disappeared.

Harriet pushed her way past the students and jogged to the airship. She prayed that the perpetrator was, indeed, a Green. She would rather face a thousand Greens than be forced to execute someone she cared for.

Before entering the dirigible, she turned her gaze skyward. The clouds were a bright pink. The sun was going down. Darkness was falling upon Oregon.

****

Harriet dipped her pounded yam into the egusi stew and slid the mixture into her mouth. “Mm, this is delicious, Mary!”

Stagecoach Mary smiled. “I told you, this is the best African restaurant in all of Oregon.

“You might just be right, but there is this place near the Gate that'll make you...”

“Excuse the interruption.”

Harriet looked over her shoulder. “Pei-Pei! Have you come to join us?”

“I wish that was the case,” Pei answered. “But a Stonecoat has breached the Wall near South Gate.”

“A *Stonecoat*? I ain't seen one of those in years!” Harriet said, rising from her chair. “This should be fun; the last one took out fifteen Union Soldiers and a Russian steambot before I could put it down."

"Count me in!" Mary said, wiping the corners of her mouth with a handkerchief.

"Then let's go, y'all," Harriet said, heading for the restaurant's exit. "We got a monster to kill!"

****

The Gate was abuzz with activity.

And soaked in blood.

The Constables who worked the top of the Gate, and the dirigibles that gave them support, fired volley after volley of 'quake-shot' at what appeared to be a colossal stone statue.

This immense effigy, however, was alive and, with the pile of pulverized Constables at its feet, apparently out for blood.

The creature stood nearly two stories tall. It appeared to be carved from gray granite with onyx striations defining its muscular frame. The creature roared as the quake-shot rocked its frame with powerful seismic tremors, but it continued to pile dead Constables atop one another.

"Gods!" Pei-Pei gasped. "So, *that's* a Stonecoat, huh?"

"Yep," Harriet replied. "Twenty feet of bone crushin' death...stronger than fifty men; bullet proof; and as ornery as a dog with a bad tooth."

"How did you kill that thing?" Constable Kojoe asked.

"Note that they are called Stone*coats*," Stagecoach Mary said. "Their hide is as hard as granite, but their insides are flesh – as soft as yours."

"And yours?" Pei replied, perusing Mary's muscular frame.

Mary shook her head. "Naw, my innards 'bout as tough as my outtards."

"How did you get to those organs, though, Harriet?" Pei-Pei Ming inquired.

"Up the fundament," Harriet said.

"Harriet put the *fun* in fundament!" Black Mary snickered.

"Eww," Pei-Pei Ming replied, turning up her nose.

"Don't be too disgusted, child," Harriet said with a smirk. "This is *your* kill."

“I would much rather observe a master at work,” Pei-Pei said.

“I bet you would,” Harriet replied. “But what kind of example would I be if I denied you the experience of your first Stonecoat kill? Besides, imagine the respect you’ll get.”

Mary dropped a firm hand on Pei’s shoulder. “Hell, you’ll probably get a promotion.”

“I guess,” Pei-Pei sighed.

“Praise the Lawd! Harriet said. “Constable, bring us down.”

Constable Kojoe, who had eagerly volunteered to pilot the airship, lowered the dirigible until it hovered just a few feet over the heads of the Constables who manned the quake cannons atop the great wall.

Harriet slid the dirigible’s mahogany door open. “Pei-Pei, use the displacement engine to touch down between the Stonecoat’s feet. We’ll distract it. When you get a chance, you know where to go.”

“Will it smell really badly?” Pei-Pei asked, her face twisted into a scowl.

“Well, it ain’t a garden of roses in there, child,” Harriet said. “Once you’re...inside, destroy as many organs as you can and then use the displacement engine to 'pop' out of there."

"Understood," Pei-Pei replied. "See you soon."

Pei-Pei leapt out of the door and then vanished.

"Kojoe," Harriet said, slamming the door shut. "Circle around to the Stonecoat's right...at about its eye-level."

"I'm on it!" Constable Kojoe replied.

"It don't have any peripheral vision, so it will have to turn its head toward us to attack us," Mary said. "That should give Pei-Pei time to do her thing."

"How quick is that thing?" Constable Kojoe asked.

"Quick enough to swat this airship like a fly if you don't shake it," Harriet answered. "But the Lawd gon' see us through."

Constable Kojoe pulled a napkin from the rear pocket of his trousers and wiped sweat from his brow. He then turned the dirigible's steering wheel to his left and slammed his foot on the pedal beneath his right foot. The dirigible hissed and then lurched forward.

On the ground below, Pei-Pei appeared, then vanished and appeared and then vanished again, avoiding the frightening, battering ram strikes of the Stonecoat. With each miss, the Stonecoat's wrecking ball-sized fists beat a crater into the soft earth.

The dirigible soared around to the side of the Stonecoat's head.

Harriet stepped behind Constable Kojoe and peered out of the windshield. She placed a firm but gentle hand on his shoulder. "Get his attention."

The constable wrapped his fingers around a brass toggle on the dashboard and then yanked his fist back toward his ribcage.

A hissing din, like the lamentation of an immense snake, erupted from the undercarriage of the dirigible. A moment later, a black, iron rocket shot from the dirigible and sped toward the Stonecoat's ear, leaving a white tail of steam behind it.

The rocket disappeared inside the Stonecoat's ear.

The creature roared in agony and staggered sideways. Smoke billowed from the Stonecoat's ear. It snapped its head toward its attacker, raising its mighty stone hand in preparation for an attack of its own.

The Stonecoat swept the back of its hand toward the airship.

"Hold tight!" Constable Kojoe shouted. He then slammed the ignition lever forward, shutting off the steam power to the engines and propellers.

The dirigible plummeted toward the earth, just avoiding the Stonecoat's powerful backhand strike.

Constable Kojoe yanked the ignition lever backward. The airship continued to fall.

"Uh oh," Harriet croaked.

"Aw, damn!" Mary sighed.

"I got this," Constable Kojoe whispered, blinking away the sweat in his eyes.

The dirigible coughed and sputtered and then came to life with a jerk, hovering, for a second, a yard above the ground before rising skyward again.

"Whew," Mary said, wiping her brow with the back of her hand. "That was closer than two cockroaches on a bread crumb!"

"Did the Gatekeeper make it in?"

Constable Kojoe asked.

Harriet slid the door open and peered downward. There was no trace of Pei-Pei. The Stonecoat clutched at its belly.

"It appear so."

An odd noise, like gravel raining upon a block of ice, rose from the Stonecoat's throat.

A torrent of a dark brown, oily substance fell from between the Stonecoat's legs and splashed at its feet. The oil filled the air with an odor like rusted iron.

The creature's coal gray eyes rolled backward and then it collapsed onto its face with a loud thud. It shuddered violently for a moment and then lay still.

Pei-Pei appeared, covered in oil and pieces of black flesh, between the Stonecoat's legs. She wiped the sludge from her face and flicked it off of her fingers to the ground.

Laughter erupted from atop the wall.

"Bring us down, Constable," Harriet said, smiling.

Constable Kojoe landed the dirigible a few yards from the Stonecoat's head.

Harriet leapt from the dirigible and sauntered toward Pei-Pei. “Good job, Gatekeeper!”

“Then why is everyone laughing?” Pei-Pei asked.

“Because you ventured up a Stonecoat’s ass,” Mary chuckled. “It would have been much easier... and less messy...to enter through its mouth!”

“But you said...” Pei-Pei began.

“Gatekeepers...let’s welcome, our sister, Pei-Pei Ming,” Harriet shouted, interrupting her. “Her initiation done. Let it be written upon y’all scrolls and sang about forever!”

“And *ever*!” Harriet’s fellow Gatekeepers shouted in reply.

“Great,” Pei-Pei Ming sighed.

“I would hug you,” Harriet said. “But...”

More laughter came from the gate.

Harriet inspected the craters formed by the Stonecoat’s punches. The ones made with its right fist were a foot deep. Those made with its left were nearly a foot and a half deep. Harriet whistled and shook her head.

"Lawd! Come on, I'll show you where to clean up, child," she said, walking toward the gate. "We have some new clothes for you, too. Hurry up and get dressed; we have to high tail it over to Tipi Wowahwa."

****

Harriet looked down through a porthole. A herd of wild horses galloped across the vast, green plains that comprised the Tipi Wowahwa District.

The dirigible landed just outside of a small village of tipi, which were constructed of buffalo skin dyed red and indigo.

"Wabli Ska and his followers live here, but so do several elders and children," Harriet said, firing up her monowheel, which was parked at the door of the airship. "Hopefully, things won't get violent, but if they do, try hard to keep collateral damage to a minimum, Mary."

Mary peered out of the porthole next to the door. "Oh, things gettin' violent is highly likely."

Harriet slid open the door. About fifty yards away – sitting atop white warhorses – were several men and women. Front and center – sitting atop a jet-black horse – was Wabli Ska. "I count thirty, in addition to Wabli Ska. We should be able to take them, but expect a few bumps and bruises."

"A few bumps and bruises?" Pei Ming echoed, raising an eyebrow. "Umm..."

"Do you need me to come?" Constable Kojoe shouted from the pilot's seat.

"No," Harriet replied. "Too many 'Law Dogs' will just set these warriors off. Just keep this bird fired up!"

Harriet revved the engine of the monowheel and exploded out of the door.

Black Mary somersaulted out behind her.

Pei vanished, reappearing ten yards – her limit with each displacement – from the airship. She vanished again, reappearing after another ten yards. Pei repeated this process until she appeared beside Mary and Harriet, who now stood beside her monowheel about five yards from Wabli Ska.

The warhorses were decorated in war-paint. Scarlet circles were painted around the animals' eyes and nostrils; and green hand prints were drawn upon each horse's hip. Each horse had a small leather medicine bag weaved into its bridle and black-tipped eagle feathers braided into its forelock and tail.

The warriors wore deerskin shirts and

trousers. Their cheeks bore a red and crimson stripe and all but Wabli Ska wore two eagle feathers sewn into their hair.

Wabli wore a bonnet made of black eagle feathers with a white tip.

“Evenin’, Wabli.” Harriet said, raising her hand in greeting.

“Good evening,” Wabli answered. “Why are you here, Harriet?”

“We have two murders on our hands,” Harriet replied. “One is a Chinese monk; the other one is a Negro girl. The Chinese symbols for war were carved into the girl’s back.”

“What has any of that got to do with me?” Wabli said. “Or you, for that matter? Since when does a monster-hunter work for the Law?”

“It could be a Green committing these crimes, but before we head out to the Green Lands, we need to weigh all of our options,” Harriet replied.

“And I’m an option? Wabli spat. “Get your ass out of here, Harriet, before you get yourself hurt!”

“We just want to talk, Wabli,” Harriet said. “You know me; you don’t want your people to die and I don’t want to hurt anyone, but if you make a move, I'll kill you all."

"I always wanted to see if you were as bad-ass as they say," a young warrior shouted. "Let me handle this, Chief!"

"Boy, shut up when grown folks are talking!" Wabli commanded. "I watched this woman kill two Wendigo with nothing but that damned shotgun on her back. You are not gonna fight her..."

Wabli threw the tomahawk at Harriet's head. "*We* are!"

Harriet dropped to one knee as she drew her shotgun. The tomahawk whizzed by her left ear.

Mary drew both of her Colt Dragoon revolvers and fired. Two warriors slumped over in their saddles, blood pouring from their foreheads.

Pei-Pei Ming vanished. A moment later, she appeared, sitting behind the young warrior who asked to fight Harriet. Pei grabbed his chin with one hand and the crest of his head with the other and then twisted forcefully. The young man fell from his horse and landed on his chest. His head – now turned backward – stared up at Pei with dead eyes.

Harriet fired a volley from her shotgun, blowing three warriors off their horses before they could string an arrow on their bows. She then leapt toward Wabli and struck him in the chest with the butt of the shotgun.

Wabli tumbled off the horse and landed, with a thud, onto his back. He recovered quickly, however, rolling to his feet and running toward the airship.

"He's going for the airship," Harriet shouted. "Stop him, Pei, but don't kill him. We need to question him. Mary and me will clean up here."

Pei nodded as she crushed a warrior's windpipe with a swift chop. She vanished, leaving Harriet and Mary to deal with the warriors.

Harriet leapt high into the air as she fired the shotgun. A warrior's head disappeared in a cloud of red mist.

She landed – rolling to avoid a volley of arrows – and then popped to her feet, squeezing the shotgun's trigger in rapid succession.

Five more warrior's fell.

The remaining warriors turned their horses around and retreated toward the village.

Mary grabbed Wabli's horse by its hind legs and hurled it at the fleeing warriors. Three were crushed under the horses weight.

Harriet hopped on her monowheel and headed back to the airship. She arrived to find Wabli face down on the ground in handcuffs. Pei stood over him.

Mary sprinted to Harriet's side, her steam-powered leg hissing in time with her rapid breaths. "That was fun!"

"Wabli, did you kill the monk and the girl?" Harriet asked.

"Yes," Wabli confessed.

Harriet was stunned. "I'll ask again..."

"No need," Wabli said, interrupting her. "I did it."

"Wabli, your father..."

"Don't mention my father!" Wabli hissed. "Just...don't...please."

"Okay, Wabli," Harriet said, pulling him to his feet. Let's go."

****

"I am so sorry, Chief Constable," Harriet said, taking a seat in front of Chief Constable

Magaska Hota's desk. "I know how close you and Wabli are."

"Yes, it saddens me," the Chief Constable said. "But I am also happy the murderer has been brought to justice."

Pei-Pei Ming handed Chief Constable Magaska Hota a form and a pen. "We just need you to sign the Writ of Execution and we will carry out the sentence."

The Chief Constable took the pen in his left hand and signed the form. "Please, make it quick. I don't want my son to suffer."

"You misunderstand, Chief," Harriet said. "Please read the name on the Writ carefully."

The Chief Constable perused the form. "Is this a joke?"

"No joke, sir," Harriet replied.

"Why is *my* name on this Writ?" The Chief Constable inquired.

"Because *you* the murderer," Harriet replied. "Shi Yan Bo suffered rib fractures to his right side; that tell me it was from a powerful *left*-legged strike. The damage on the left side of his neck came from an attack from behind, with the killer's left hand."

Harriet stood up. "The girl got defensive wounds on her right forearm, caused by a razor attack with the killer's left hand...and just now, you signed the Writ with yo' left hand, but when Wabli attacked me, he threw the tomahawk with his right hand."

"You have a good son, former Chief Constable," Pei-Pei Ming said. "He would rather die than see it happen to his father."

"Oh, please," Magaska Hota hissed, staring down at his desk. "He just wants to be a martyr. The fool thinks it will further his cause."

Harriet drew her shotgun. "If you look up from that paper...if you move your head one inch, you'll lose it."

Magaska Hota laughed gleefully and clapped his hand. "Oh, you *are* a smart one, aren't you? You know what I am. Very good."

"Yeah, the Lawd done made it clear," Harriet said. "You a Two-Face. The Stonecoat was a lefty, too, by the way. I guess all you Greens is."

Harriet did not take her eyes – or her weapon – off of the monster as she addressed Pei Ming. "Pei-Pei, the gaze of a Two-Face paralyzes so it can drain its victims' blood without them putting up a fight. They also like to cause war and strife...easier for them to hunt during the chaos."

"She can't read a lick, but she's smart!" Magaska Hota chuckled.

"What I don't know is how you took possession of the Chief without breaching the Wall," Harriet said, ignoring the Two-Face's taunts.

"I have been with Magaska Hota since his family brought him here when he was twelve," the creature replied. "I – of course – had to lay dormant in my host for quite a while before I could take over. During that time, the boy got married and conceived a son. Wabli and Magaska Hota were very close by the time I took over and Wabli noticed the change. I guess he hoped that his death would shock Magaska Hota into waking up and casting me out, but it's too late. Magaska Hota's soul is dead."

"That's all I needed to know." Harriet pulled the trigger.

The Two-Face's head was blown from its shoulders. A greenish-black ichor spewed from the creature's neck. Its headless body shuddered and then collapsed onto the floor.

"He is going to cry," Pei Ming sighed.

“Wabli Ska?” Harriet asked.

Pei shook her head. “No…the janitor when he sees this mess he has to clean up.”

“I’ll give him a few leaves of that funny smellin’ tobacco Mary keeps hidden in her bag,” Harriet said. “That’ll put a smile on his face.”

“I just teleported up a Stonecoat’s backside,” Pei-Pei replied. I could use something to make me smile, too.”

“Then, come on child,” Harriet said, walking toward the door. “Next stop…*Mary’s* place.”

CHAPTER FOUR

September 19, 1870

Kraken's Almanac belched a cloud of steam into the air, high above the docks at the Port of Dover. John Brown sauntered down the ramp onto the dock, carrying a worn, leather suitcase. In the distance loomed the steam train of the South Eastern Railway.

There's our ride," Brown whispered.

Caleb squirmed under his vest. "Let's shake a leg, then!"

John Brown sprinted toward the train.

"All aboard!" The conductor shouted as he stepped up into the train.

Brown leapt into the train behind him.

The conductor turned to face Brown with his hand extended. “Your ticket, sir?”

“I am a representative of Professor Kleinhopper,” Brown replied.

“Ah, yes. We were expecting you a bit earlier,” the conductor said. “Welcome to England!”

“Thanks,” John Brown said. “Could you kindly tell me where my seat is? I’m mighty tired.”

“Certainly, sir,” the conductor replied, signaling John Brown to follow with a wave of his hand. “Right this way.”

The conductor led him through two coach cars filled with passengers who smelled of cheap cigars and Earl Grey, past the dining car and into a car lined with maroon velvet, an oxblood leather couch and chair and a hand-carved mahogany table.

“Here you are, sir,” the conductor said. “Lunch will be served shortly. I hope your car is to your liking.”

“It is,” John Brown replied, smiling. “Thank you.”

The conductor bowed slightly and then left the car.

"Lemme see," Caleb said.

John Brown unbuttoned his vest and one button of his shirt. Caleb peeked out and perused the room. He whistled in approval. "That nigger's got class!"

"Unlike you!" Brown hissed. "Must you always be so vulgar?"

"My apologies," Caleb said. "I forgot you was a nigger...I mean *negro*-lover. But when we kill this other nigger...excuse me...*negro*, Baas Bello, you will not be bothered with my vulgar ass much longer."

"We cannot get to Whitechapel soon enough." John Brown sighed.

The train ride continued on in silence. John Brown did not dislike Caleb, but he resented him because, while Caleb's ability to infect others was still active, his power to possess was not. The moment they were separated, he would possess Banneker and use his wealth, resources and army of knolls to topple the United States government and finally build his Black nation, over which he would rule. He, of course, would have Harriet and Black Mary hunted down and executed. They were the cause of his hellish marriage to Caleb – it was either that, or die – they had thwarted him at every turn and he wanted justice at any cost.

John Brown exited the train at its stop in the East End of London, in the Borough of Tower Hamlets. Outside of the station was a line of horse-drawn carriages. Each driver wore a black, wool Inverness coat and a black top-hat. Except for one man, who wore a smaller John Bull top-hat with a red band and sported a red velvet smoking jacket.

"That's the one," Brown said, walking toward the carriage.

The carriage driver peered down at him.

"For Professor Kleinhopper," Brown said with a nod.

The driver pulled back on an iron lever that extended from the floor next to his right shin. The carriage door opened.

John slid his suitcase onto the top of the carriage and then climbed inside it. He sat back and enjoyed the coolness of the plush leather against his back and thighs.

The carriage took off. John Brown stared out the window. What he saw disturbed him. On the streets and alleys of the East End, hordes of urchins toiled. They were ragged and filthy, their feet bare; their expressions, grave and careworn. For these children, life was nothing but hard work, empty bellies and the constant struggle for survival. Much like the enslaved Black people in America. *"After I have built my Black Empire, perhaps we will storm the East End and make it a better place,"* Brown thought.

The carriage came to a smooth halt.

"Whitechapel!" The carriage driver shouted.

John Brown stepped out of the carriage. The driver handed him his luggage and then rode off.

"How are we going to find this damned Spirit-Engine?" Caleb whispered, peering out from the space made by the vest button John Brown left undone. "This place is just one big mess of filth and factories."

"Baas Bello is wealthy and, most importantly, Black," John Brown replied. "He would not find many safe spaces among these people. Where, however, can a man with money – regardless of his race, color or creed – go and be shown some measure of respect and even loyalty, if he's willing to pay for it?"

"God damn, Brown, you're a genius!" Caleb said. "That old bastard hid it in a brothel!"

"I'd wager he did," John Brown said.

"But in Whitechapel, whorehouses outnumber churches," Caleb said. It's gonna take us forever and a day to find the one."

"Then we had best get started," John Brown replied.

CHAPTER FIVE

Harriet and Mary crept across the wood-paved alleyway to a high fence made of oak, the shadows of the night providing cover for their movement. Harriet leapt over the fence. Mary followed her, her mechanical leg releasing a soft hiss. The women darted up the back stairs of the three-story wooden house. Harriet tapped on the door three times. She paused for a second and tapped twice more. She paused again and then tapped a final time.

The back door opened a crack. Harriet slipped inside. Mary opened the door a bit wider and darted into the house. Baas Bello greeted them with warm hugs. He smiled, but to Harriet, his eyes revealed worry, something uncommon for the immortal genius.

"Harriet! Mary! It is so good to see you!"

"You talk like you ain't laid eyes on us in years, Baas," Harriet said. "It's only been four months. What's eatin' you?"

"Come, sit down and let's talk," Baas said, turning on his heels. He looked over his shoulder as he walked down the hallway. "I have already prepared chai for you. I added cream and sugar just the way you like it, Harriet and Mary, I added your preferred shot of Kentucky Bourbon."

"Good old Baas!" Mary said, clapping her hands.

Harriet and Mary followed Baas into a room with walls built from ebony bookshelves. Thousands of books, in several languages, filled every slot in each of the four walls. At the center of the room was a round, ebony table with four matching chairs. On the table sat three white, tea cups.

Baas pointed at one of the cups. "Harriet."

Harriet sat down, lifted the cup to her lips and took a sip. The cinnamon and ginger in the tea warmed her. "It's good, Baas. As always.

"Thank you," Baas replied. "Mary?"

Stagecoach Mary sat down and took a long

swig. She handed the empty cup to Baas. "That was mighty tasty, Baas. Add a little bit more bourbon to the next round, if you please."

Baas laughed. "I'll be right back."

He exited the room, returned a minute later with another cup of chai for Mary and then sat down at the table.

"First, thank you for your work in Oregon," he said. "Oregon is my grand experiment to see if the people of this land can work together when our various cultures are allowed to be practiced and are equally valued. So far, so good."

"So far," Harriet replied. "But the Greens outside the Gate are becoming more active and more breaches are bound to happen soon."

"After this war, I would like for the three of us to settle there," Baas said. "To protect and help govern it."

"I like Oregon," Mary said. "The food is good; the liquor is strong. Count me in!"

Harriet shook her head. "Lawd, Mary! Well, if the Lawd show me it's time for me to settle, I'll settle, but soldierin' is all I know. Anyhow, what is goin' on Baas?"

"I'm in trouble," Baas said. "Banneker has

struck a bargain with John Brown and Caleb. They have headed to Whitechapel in London to find one of my creations – a thousand year old device I call the Spirit-Engine."

"What does the Alchemist need that fo'?" Harriet inquired.

"To kill me," Baas answered. "The Spirit-Engine allows travel to a reality nearly identical to our own – a reality where no one possesses special gifts like we do here. No one, except me, that is."

"So, nobody like me or Harriet to watch your back over there." Mary said.

"You already understand, then," Baas said.

"Yeah," Harriet said. "But what would killin' that world's Baas have to do with you?"

Baas sipped his tea before he spoke. "We are all linked to our double in that reality. When one of us dies here, our double dies there and vice versa. Most of us are unaware of our double. My double and I are fully aware of each other's surface thoughts and activities."

Harriet shook her head. "Lawd! So, how can we help Baas?"

"Harriet, I need you to travel to that

alternate world and stop Brown and Caleb if you can," Baas said. "Finding the Spirit-Engine won't be easy and finding my double will be even harder, so even though they are several days ahead of you, you may well be able to intercept and stop them."

Harriet nodded. "Consider it, done."

"What about me, Baas?" Mary asked.

"Mary, the Spirit-Engine tears apart any non-immortal who uses it," Baas replied. "That is why Banneker has not sent his knolls after my double."

"But Caleb and John Brown ain't immortals," Mary said.

"No, but Caleb's fluid nature will allow him to reform after his disintegration," Baas replied. "As will Harriet's regenerative powers."

"My tough hide can take it, Baas," Mary said. "We can't send Harriet to a whole 'nother world all by her lonesome."

"We have no choice," Baas said. "I feel so helpless already. Please, do not make me feel worse."

"It's okay, Baas," Harriet said. "We know you ain't no coward. Me goin' makes mo' sense. And Mary, this war is what I was born fo'. The

Lawd done made me his soldier and I'm pledged to serve him unto my death...in this world and any other one."

Mary swallowed her second cup of tea. "This don't sit well with me."

"If Harriet falls and I am killed," Baas sighed. "Mary, I'll need you here to take up the fight against Banneker until Harriet returns and joins you."

Mary nodded.

"Alright then, it's settled," Baas said. "Rest up, we leave for Whitechapel at dawn."

CHAPTER SIX

September 21, 1870

John Brown stood at the corner of Whitechapel Road and Dorset Street – described as "the worst street in London" – pulling at his beard as he perused the dwellings around him – dwellings called *Blackwall Buildings*, because they belonged to Blackwall Railway, housed most of the prostitutes who worked the brothels – 62 of them by John Brown's count – in Whitechapel. Sitting outside of one building was a little boy with rosy cheeks and dead, gray eyes that looked as if they had never seen a sunrise, or lovers holding hands, or the filth all around them.

John Brown crept toward the boy.

"May I help you, sir?" The boy asked.

"Are you really blind boy?" Brown inquired. "How did you know I was here?"

"You ain't as quiet as you would imagine, sir," the boy replied.

"Your name Bertrand Plummer?"

"Yes, sir."

"Well, Bert, I am told that if it happens in Whitechapel, you know about it. If you can give me some helpful information, I will pay you a pound for your trouble," John Brown said. "If the information is not so helpful, I will still pay you ten shillings for your time."

Bert rose from his seat. "Ask away, then, sir! I will do my best to give you a proper answer."

Brown laid a hand on Bert's shoulder. "Son, I have been searching for a place where a man of a...darker persuasion might frequent for the company and comfort of a woman."

"A darker persuasion? You mean a Fuzzy, sir?" Bert asked.

"Yes," John Brown answered. "But an *educated* Fuzzy, with a bit of a Moorish accent."

"There was a man like that 'round here once or twice, sir," Bert said. "He stayed a couple of days at *Mama Koko's* a few years back. Nice man, for a Fuzzy. Bought a sandwich and soup for me and me mum and ain't ask for nothin' in return."

"*Mama Koko's* on Thrawl Street?"

"That be the very one, sir."

John Brown grabbed Bert's hand, placed two large coins in it and closed his fist around them.

"There's two pounds for you," John Brown said. "You were very helpful, son."

Bert smiled. "Thank you, sir! Me mum and me will eat good for a few days and maybe she can stay off her back for a day or two, too!"

"Let's hope so," John Brown said, turning on his heels.

"God bless you, sir!" Bert shouted.

John brown strode up Whitechapel Road, toward Thrawl. Within a few minutes, he had arrived at the door of Mama Koko's. As he was about to knock, the door opened. A beautiful woman – clad in only a red corset, a matching dress that stopped at her thighs and a gold ring on her left middle toe – stood before John Brown. By the look of her long brown hair, dark tan and almond-shaped eyes, Brown figured she was of Asian and Caucasian descent.

"Come in, love," she said. "I'm Madame Koko, but you can call me Mama."

Her accent was strange, something Brown had never heard before. He stepped inside.

"Your voice is beautiful," John Brown said, "But very unique. May I ask where you are from?"

"My mother is Sicilian," Madame Koko replied. "My father is part Blackamoor; part Arab – from Egypt. I was born and raised in Cairo."

"Ah, no wonder Baas Bello found this place so welcoming, then," John Brown said.

Madame Koko's face was stone, but a single rivulet of sweat crept down her brow. "I am sorry, I have never heard of this person."

Madame Koko tried to walk away, but John Brown grabbed her arm. "I believe you have."

Two men, both nearly seven feet tall, heavily muscled, with matching mugs obviously forged in many boxing and catch wrestling rings, darted from out of the shadows, placing their bullish bodies between John Brown and Mama Koko. Brown's hand was yanked off of the madam's arm. Mama Koko strutted into the parlor, where a dozen men and two dozen women laughed, drank and cuddled.

"Evenin' gents," one of the twins said with a tip of his bowler. "Me name's Connor and this handsome bloke is me brother, Colin. Afraid you will have to leave our fine establishment now, or we'll be forced to batty-fang ya'."

A muffled din erupted from under John Brown's vest. "We'll leave when we get what we came for!"

Connor and Colin exchanged quick glances.

"How'd you say that without openin' your sauce-box?" Colin asked.

"Wasn't me," John Brown replied.

Brown yanked his vest open, sending the buttons flying in all directions.

Caleb flashed a wide grin at the twins. "It was me!"

The twins hopped backward in unison.

"What the bloody hell?" Connor gasped.

"Damfino!" Colin croaked. *"Damned if I know."*

"You...you're the Devil!" Colin wailed.

"Not quite," Caleb replied. "But we shol' 'nuff 'bout to send you to Hell!"

John Brown's face turned soft and claylike, oozing like hot wax. His mouth formed into a gaping hole, filled with several spiraling rows of needle-like teeth. In place of his eyes and ears were smaller mouths identical to the large one.

A tendril of thick flesh carrying Caleb's face shot out of John Brown's torso. Caleb sank his teeth into Colin's thigh and then the tendril retracted back into John Brown's torso.

Colin fell to the floor, screaming in agony as blood poured down his pants leg.

Caleb spit. A pink chunk of flesh and a patch of Colin's brown cotton trousers landed between Connor's feet.

"Tastes like chicken!" Caleb chuckled.

John Brown exploded forward, closing on Connor, his spine making strange clicking noises as he encircled the big man like a boa constrictor trapping it's pray. As Brown's malleable frame slithered about Connor, his many mouths tore at the man's flesh, opening dozens of deep wounds. The mouths that were once John Brown's eyes chewed at Connor's throat, severing his vocal cords.

Brown released Connor and he fell beside his brother, writhing in silence.

Panic spread through the brothel like a plague. Patrons and prostitutes alike rushed toward the door, but were cut down by the teeth of the John Brown / Caleb hybrid. The creature's arms and legs were now tendrils, lined with scores of biting mouths that captured and bit chunks out of all in their path.

Blood, flesh and entrails painted the walls of the parlor and other rooms on the first floor. The John Brown / Caleb creature then slithered up the stairs to the second floor, where it found several prostitutes hiding with their terrified clients. The creature tore them apart with relish, ensuring to deliver killing bites to major arteries as they did on the floor below – neither Brown nor Caleb wanted an army of Ghul whores and whoremongers terrorizing London.

Within a quarter hour, everyone in the brothel was dead.

John Brown and Caleb resumed their "human" form and searched the top floor, going from room to room, looking for a false wall or hidden door.

All of the rooms were identical and clean, except for the bloody mess they had just made.

In one room, however, John Brown found a cobweb in the corner. He searched the items in the room – a chest-of-drawers, a bed, a chair and a wash basin – and found a bit of dust on the chest and on the seat of the chair, as if the room had not been used in quite some time.

John pounded on the walls, they sounded solid. He stomped on the hardwood floor, it too, was solid. He looked under thc bed. A blanket and a woman's wool coat were folded neatly on the floor. John slid the bed aside and then tossed the blanket and coat onto it. He stomped on the floor where the blanket and coat once lay and was rewarded with an echo, as if the floor beneath was hollow.

John pulled at a plank of wood with his fingers and it came up easily. He removed another plank and another, exposing a gray, metal door beneath the wood. In the center of the door was a ring.

John twisted the ring clockwise until he heard a click and then he released the ring. The door slid open, revealing an iron ladder that descended into darkness. The smell of feces and urine billowed up from the dank blackness.

"Damn!" Caleb said. "What in the hell is makin' that stink?"

"I suppose we are about to find out," John

Brown replied, placing one foot on the ladder.

"'Spose so," Caleb said.

John Brown descended the ladder, disappearing into shadow, like a ship slipping below the surface of murky waters.

John Brown broke through the smothering darkness just as his feet touched cold stone.

He stood in a capacious room that was dimly lit by four indigo spheres – one in each corner – that glowed with a soft light.

In the center of the room, about thirty feet away, sat a large machine, from which several wires and tubes protruded. Sitting atop the machine was another indigo sphere, but this one glowed more intensely than the others.

"That must be the Spirit-Engine," Caleb said. "You ready, old man?"

"As ready as I will ever be, I suppose," John replied.

A soft chuckle came from the other side of the men.

"What the hell?" Caleb whispered.

"Who's there?" John Brown asked, craning

his neck toward the machine.

The sound of shuffling feet and metal dragged across stone answered.

“Show yourself!” John Brown demanded.

A man, if you can call it that, stepped out from behind the machine. He stood nearly six feet tall, but his legs were the length of a boy not quite in his teens. The creature stood with its sinewy arms hanging at its sides, its knuckles scraping the floor. His long, thick torso swayed back and forth as if he was intoxicated. The man’s eyes were dark and penetrating. In contrast, his smile was warm and bright.

The man darted forward.

Shocked by the sudden and aggressive movement, John Brown crouched low with his fists raised.

“Hello, there, gents,” the man said, stopping a foot from John Brown. “Jack Springheels, at your service. I would welcome you with a handshake, but alas, I cannot reach you. Why don’t you come a bit closer?”

John Brown looked toward the floor. Around Jack’s left ankle was a thick, iron chain that extended from a slot carved into and around the center of the engine.

"My name is Brown; John Brown," Brown said. "Why are you here? Why are you in chains?"

"Been here 880 years, has I," Jack replied. "Got 120 more to go and Bello lets me go."

"You're Baas Bello's prisoner? Jack inquired.

Jack shook his head. "His employee. I protects his engine. No one goes through or comes out and lives unless Bello tell me face-to-face."

"I have come a very long way to use the Spirit-Engine," Brown said. " Let me use it unmolested and I will bring you back a feast. You must be starved down here."

"Oh, I eats," Jack said. "I gets my fill of rats, roaches and the ghosts that haunts this place."

"Oh boy," Caleb said, rolling his eyes.

Jack chuckled. "It talks! Hello, belly-face. What's your name?"

"Caleb Butler," Caleb replied.

"Pleased to meet you, Caleb Butler," Jack said. "What with the 'oh boy'?"

Caleb snickered. “How can you possibly eat a ghost?”

“Well, I kills it first, of course,” Jack replied. “I ain’ts no savage!”

“You kill ghosts?” Caleb asked with a smirk.

Jack raised his hands before his face; claws, as long as daggers, extended from them. “With these, I can cut and kills anything – iron, glass, ghosts, goblins, and even the Good Lord hisself should I one day have the pleasure of his acquaintance.”

“Then, why not cut the chains and free yourself?” John Brown asked.

“They’s enchanted,” Jack said. “By Bello witchery. Only the intestines of a white man can break the enchantment. You the first white mens been down here in ever.”

“Leave us be and we will bring you a white man’s intestines upon our return,” John Brown said.

Jack’s smile grew wider. “Why wait? You here already.”

Jack struck with lightning speed, the claws of his hands digging into both sides of John Brown’s ribcage.

Brown and Caleb screamed in unison.

Jack pulled his hands toward his chest. The ripping force separated the men. A naked Caleb stumbled backward and then fell, landing on his haunches. John Brown was still caught in Jack's grip. Jack brought both arms forcefully upward and outward above his shoulders, tearing John Brown in half as easily as a man rips a piece of tissue.

Jack opened his mouth wide, letting a torrent of blood rain inside his gaping maw.

Caleb crawled to the front of the Spirit-Engine. There was a brass lever protruding from a bronze plate on the machine's face. Caleb grabbed the handle and snatched it downward. The light at the top of the machine went black.

Jack dropped the halves of John Brown onto the floor. "No!"

A vertical chasm, glowing bright violet, opened in the air to Caleb's left. He leapt to his feet and sprinted toward it.

Jack was hot on Caleb's heels, slashing furiously with his claws.

Caleb leapt through the chasm. Jack's claws just missing the back of his neck.

The chasm closed. The light on top of the

Spirit-Engine came back on.

"I am in so much troubles!" Jack sobbed. "Bello never lets me go, now!"

Jack stared at John Brown's torn and tattered body. A smile stretched from one cheek to the other.

"Intestines," he whispered. "A *white* man intestines!"

CHAPTER SEVEN

The Nefertiti landed, silently, upon *Mama Koko's* roof. Baas pressed a pedal with his right foot and the airship's giant balloon deflated, folding in upon itself until it was in a neat rectangle that rested atop *the Nefertiti.*

"Baas, this airship gon' go crashin' through the roof of this place!" Harriet whispered.

"The roof is fortified," Baas said. "It could hold *two* airships comparable to *the Nefertiti's* weight."

Mary wrapped a burly arm around Baas' waist and then leapt out of the airship. She landed with a dull thud.

Harriet landed behind her without making a sound. She looked up at the sign above the door. “Mama Koko’s Oasis. What kind of place is this, Baas?”

Mary laughed. “You know what kind of place it is, Harriet. Baas...you old whoremonger, you!”

Baas’ dark brown face reddened. “I assure you, I am no whoremonger. I simply use this as a hiding place for the Spirit-Engine. No one would suspect it is here.”

Harriet pressed her fist to her hip and frowned. “No one would have suspected it was in church, either.”

Mary threw up her hands. “Amen!”

“Or in a inn,” Harriet continued. “Or on a riverboat; or at...”

“Alright!” Baas said, interrupting her. “Please...we have to stay alert.”

“Oh, we alert, Baas,” Mary replied. “We *wide* awake, now.”

Baas tugged at his cravat. “Anyway...umm...right now we have much to do; we will discuss this later.”

“Harriet nodded. “We sho’ will.”

Mary laughed, but her laughter quickly faded. She sniffed the air. “Blood,” she whispered. “A lot of it. All over the brothel.”

Harriet drew the *Bello Mule* and then aimed it at the door.

Mary drew both Colt Dragoon revolvers and held them at the ready.

Baas checked the door, pressing his palm against it. The door creaked open.

Harriet crept inside, with Mary and Baas close behind her.

“Lawd,” Harriet sighed as she studied the grisly scene.

“Damn!” Mary said. “That John Brown-Caleb mishmash obviously beat us here.”

“They are, more than likely, dead too,” Baas said, trotting toward the stairway. “Let’s check upstairs.”

Harriet and Mary followed Baas to the second floor.

At the top of the stairs, Harriet tapped Baas on the shoulder. Baas peered over his shoulder at her.

“You said John Brown and Caleb are most

likely dead," Harriet said. "What you mean by that? A bunch of fallen women killed those monsters?"

"No," Baas replied. "In 869, I was hired by the Saracens, who lived in desert areas in and near the Roman province of Arabia, to capture one of the gifted who had been terrorizing them for over a decade, killing any woman it could find out alone and eating her entrails."

Baas continued to speak as he walked toward a room in the middle of the hallway. "I discovered that this man, whose name was Jek, had been sent by Basil I, ruler of the Byzantine Empire, to demoralize and weaken the Saracens, who had refused to bend to his rule. I used a chain nkisi to ensnare him."

"A chain inky, what?" Mary said, scratching her head.

"Nkisi," Baas replied. "In-KEE-see. An nkisi is a statue or some other container that holds medicines and a soul combined to give it life and power. When I built this place to hide the Spirit-Engine, I brought him here and tethered Jek – who now calls himself Jack – to it."

"And this Jack is powerful enough to kill John Brown and Caleb?" Harriet asked.

"Jack is the fastest creature I have ever encountered," Baas said. "And his claws could easily rend even Mary's flesh. He is cunning and brutal. Jek is a slave to his appetites, though and therein lies the way to defeat him."

"Hopefully, John Brown and Caleb didn't find the way," Harriet said.

"Let's hope not," Baas sighed.

Baas entered the room. The bed had been moved and the coat and blanket that concealed the door in the floor were on it.

"They found it," Baas said.

"Lawd!" Harriet replied.

Baas opened the metal door. "The Spirit-Engine is located in the room below. Jek is chained to it. The chain is long, but not long enough to reach you. I will go down first and assure..."

Mary shoved Baas aside. "Last one down is a rotten egg!" She leapt down the hole.

Baas rolled to his feet. "Mary is so reckless! I swear, I..."

"I gotta see this Jack befo' Mary kills him!" Harriet said before she disappeared down the hole.

Baas covered his eyes with his hand. “Why do I even bother?” He descended the ladder into the darkness. At the bottom, Harriet awaited him. Mary stood over the tattered halves of John Brown’s corpse.

“No sign of Jack,” Harriet said.

Baas ran to the chain, which was in a neat pile at the center of the room. He inspected it and found bits of flesh all over it. “Intestines! No!”

“Those probably come from John Brown, here,” Mary said. “He’s all messed up.”

“Where is Caleb?” Baas asked.

“No sign of him,” Mary replied.

“He must have used the engine, Baas,” Harriet said.

Baas slumped onto his haunches. “No. Jack is free and Caleb is now well on his way to killing my other self.”

“Guess we’d better get me over there so I can end him befo’ he succeeds,” Harriet said.

“Yes,” Baas said leaping to his feet. “Let’s hurry!”

CHAPTER EIGHT

Caleb leapt through the crack in reality and landed on the floor of the sub-basement of the brothel with a thud. A moment later, he fell to his knees and vomited. He panted heavily as he wiped the sputum from the corners of his mouth.

He struggled to his bare feet and looked around – no Jack; no Spirit-Engine; no torn apart John Brown. The room was well lit by three ormolu chandeliers, each housing nine candles. The walls of the room were perforated by hundreds of slots. Within each slot was a bottle of wine. In each corner of the room sat a barrel that, from the smell, was filled with rum.

Caleb knelt at a barrel and put his mouth

under the oak spigot. He turned the lever and then savored the spiced rum that poured into his mouth. He pushed the lever back to its original position and then lumbered toward the ladder. He ascended it, sliding the door aside at the top. Two pairs of big hands grabbed him under his armpits and yanked him off the ladder and into the room, which was empty save for a desk upon which sat several sheets of loose paper.

Colin and Connor held his arms behind his back.

"Stealin' our spirits, ay?" Colin spat. "And bare as a baby's arse, to boot. "What, were you and one of the girls tryin' to powder the hair without payin' fer it?"

Caleb shook his head. "Naw, I was just..."

"Don't sell me a dog!" Connor barked, interrupting him. "*Don't lie to me!* I can smell it all over ya'. Yer half rats, already."

Caleb smiled. "Y'all gon' make *great* soldiers in my army!"

Connor's thick brow furrowed "Your what? Are you mad?"

Caleb's arms slithered around the brothers' wrists and pulled them, kicking and screaming, into his back, which opened like a gaping maw. The twins disappeared inside Caleb's torso and his back closed. Caleb licked his lips. "Naw, not mad; just hungry."

Caleb sat on the desk, thumbing through the papers. "Nothing here about Baas Bello. Where would that nigger be? Hell, why should I care? Me and John Brown are separated now. Poor old John. But Harriet Tubman...I owe her for killin' *my* twin. Gonna find yo' double and make her pay, Harriet Tubman! You hear me? I'm gon'..."

Caleb pressed his palm to his belly. "Aw, my achin' guts! Feel like I got the backdoor trots!"

Caleb squatted. A rumbling din rose from his stomach. A moment later, a deluge of liquid feces erupted from Caleb's backside.

"What a relief!" Caleb sighed.

An ocean of excrement covered the floor of the room. Caleb smiled at his handiwork.

The ordure began to close in on itself; to become solid. Within a few minutes, the dung had formed into brown statues, roughly in the shape of Colin and Connor. The feces became more and more defined, until it had taken on the perfect form of the twins. The excrement effigies shifted and swirled, twisting and turning about on their heels until, finally, they had taken on the human flesh appearance of the twins.

Colin and Connor, now Ghuls, knelt before their king. “How may we serve?” They said in unison.

“Get me some clothes; somethin’ fancy,” Caleb replied. “And a crown. Every king needs a crown!”

CHAPTER NINE

Baas pulled the lever on the Spirit-Engine and the indigo light on top of the machine turned off. The violet chasm opened before Harriet.

"Harriet, step through the chasm, now!" Baas shouted. "You have about eight seconds before it closes. If you miss this window, we'll have to wait another hour for the engine to recharge."

Harriet leapt toward the chasm. The tear in reality seemed to pulse and then the world tilted.

"Not now, Lawd," Harriet thought.

Harriet collapsed onto the ground before the chasm.

Mary sprinted toward her. "Damn it, Harriet! You and your doggone sleepin' sickness!"

Mary snatched Harriet up from the ground and then held her at her hip like a sack of flour.

"Toss her in, Mary!" Baas said. "Quickly!"

Mary peered over her shoulder at Baas. A toothy grin was on her face. "I got a better idea."

"Mary, no!" Baas shouted. "You'll be torn asunder!"

Mary leapt through the chasm with Harriet still held aloft at her side. "My hide's too tough for all tha..."

The chasm closed.

Baas pressed his forehead against the front of the Spirit-Engine. His shoulders heaved as he sobbed. "Mary."

CHAPTER TEN

Caleb wondered if he had really gone anywhere at all. The world looked the same as before he stepped through the tear in space. Whitechapel was just as filthy as it was two days ago when he first set foot in the East End. Perhaps Banneker had played some grand trick on him for calling Banneker a nigger. Perhaps Banneker knew all along that the separation from John Brown that he promised would be at the hands of that bastard, Jack. He would be sure to get answers from Banneker once he had eaten Harriet's heart and made his way back home.

Connor and Colin stood at the intersection of Whitechapel and Dorset, keeping an eye out for trouble as Caleb sat next to Bertrand Plummer on his stoop. Bert was just as young,

Caleb observed; just as rosy cheeked; just as blind.

"I'm back for more information," Caleb said.

Bert leaned in closer to Caleb as if to hear him clearer. "Back, sir?"

"Well, I was with a man you spoke with," Caleb replied. "He paid you two pounds for information on a nig...a fuzzy who frequents *Mama Koko's.*"

"Two pounds!" Bert gasped. "I wish what you say was true, sir, but I ain't never talked to such a man. If you meet him, send him me way, if you'd be so kind, sir."

"Maybe I am *in a different world,"* Caleb thought.

Caleb patted Bert on the knee. "Well, I tell you what, if you can point me in the right direction, I guarantee I can give you new eyes. You'll be able to lay eyes on every mudsill, curly wolf and four-flusher in this outhouse y'all call a town."

"I don't speak yank, so I don't rightfully know what those things are," Bert said. "But I would sure like to see them if you be able to work that sort of magic, sir."

"I can," Caleb replied. "And I don't speak no damned Yank, neither. I'm a Southerner, through-and-through!"

"Then ask away, sir!" Bert said.

"Ever hear of a fuzzy named Bello comin' round here?"

"Bello, sir?"

"Yep. He is usually in the company of at least one woman who goes by the moniker of Harriet Tubman."

Bert sat bolt upright. "I never heard of this Mr. Bello, sir, but anybody with half a brain knows who Harriet Tubman is."

Caleb leaned forward on the stoop. "Who, pray-tell, is she?"

Bert smiled. "Why, the Vice President of Freedonia, of course."

Caleb fell back as if he had been shot. He pressed his palm to his chest. "The what of where?"

"The Vice President of Freedonia," Bert said again. "Me mum calls Freedonia the Land of the Fuzzies. Well there and their neighbor, New Haiti."

"Goddamn! I *am* in another world," Caleb whispered.

"What was that, sir," Bert inquired.

"Nothing," Caleb replied. "Thank you, for that information. Now, I'll make good on my end of the bargain."

"I'm ready, sir," Bert said, smiling.

"I doubt that," Caleb said, pointing his index fingers at Bert's dull irises.

Caleb pushed his fingers forward, slowly sinking them into Bert's eyes.

The boy wailed in agony.

Caleb drove his fingers deeper.

Bert convulsed wildly.

Caleb withdrew his fingers and Bert collapsed in a quivering heap on the ground before his stoop.

Caleb stood and sauntered toward the twins.

"Let's go," he said.

Connor handed Caleb a jewel encrusted crown. Caleb slipped the crown onto his head.

Connor and Colin took a knee before him.

"Where to, your majesty?" The twins asked.

"To the docks," Caleb answered. "We need to catch a ride on a ship."

"Yes, your majesty!" The twins said.

"Get ready, boys," Caleb said. "You're going to America!"

As they walked off, Bert sat up on his haunches. He smiled as he looked at the world for the first time. Then he frowned. He was hungry and he could not wait for his mother to return so he could have his fill...of her.

****

At the docks, Caleb spoke to the Captains and crew of several ships. All were British ships headed for India and China except for one: *the SS Savannah,* a hybrid screw propeller steamship and sailing ship. *The SS Savannah* was the first steamship credited with crossing the Atlantic Ocean between the United States and Europe. Word was it was leaving England for the United States within the hour.

"Howdy," Caleb said with a tip of his crown as he sauntered toward the *SS Savanah.* Connor and Colin lumbered behind him.

The captain of the ship ceased his

examination of the ship's manifest. He peered up from his copy-holder and smirked. "Kinda busy, your kingship. State your business, please."

Caleb continued to approach, stopping less than an arm's-length from the captain. "My name's is Caleb Butler. The gentlemen behind me are Connor and Colin."

Caleb extended his hand. The captain shook it.

"Captain Richard Hunt, at your service."

"How much would it cost for me and my compañeros to hitch a ride on your ship?" Caleb asked, still holding on to Captain Hunt's hand.

Captain Hunt thrust the manifest toward Caleb's face. Stopping a half inch from his nose. "You see this? It's the ship's manifest. We're full. We can't take one more passenger, let alone three."

Caleb pulled the captain's hand to his chest and tightened his grip. "Relax...Dick. I know, I know...you are an El Capitano. Most times, you speak to folks anyway you damned well please and they take it. But this here? This ain't one of those times."

Captain Hunt glared at Caleb, unblinking. "Release my hand right now, or..."

Caleb slapped him.

The captain's knees buckled. His scowl twisted into a mask of fear.

"Do I look like a nigger to you?" Caleb said.

"Huh?" Captain Hunt croaked.

Caleb slapped him again. Harder.

Captain Hunt collapsed onto one knee. Caleb pulled him to his feet.

"Do I look like a *nigger* to you?" Caleb repeated.

"N-no, sir," the captain cried.

"Then, don't talk to me like one!" Caleb said.

"Yes, sir."

Caleb released the captain's hand and patted him on the cheek. The captain, fearing another slap, sank his head between his shoulders.

"Now, if you'd be so kind as to show us our sleeping quarters," Caleb said. "After that, get your face checked out, looks like I scratched your cheek."

Caleb peered over his shoulder at the twins and smiled. The twins snickered.

Captain Hunt led Caleb to a large room in which there were several iron cages lining the walls. Within each cage lay a child, no younger than nine and no older than thirteen, by the looks of them. The children did not move when Caleb and the twins followed the captain into the room.

"Apologies," Captain Hunt said. "This is the only room with enough space for you. I will bring blankets, pillows and food."

"What's wrong with them?" Caleb asked, pointing at the cages.

"I...I don't know why I am telling you this..."

"That would be the scratch I gave you," Caleb said. "Welcome to the Ghul Army, son! Now, go on..."

"We have given them an herb I picked up during my travels in Southeast Asia," Captain Hunt replied. "They will sleep until they are given another herb that will awaken them..."

Caleb patted the captain on the chest with the back of his hand. "You are a bad boy, tricky Dicky! Gonna sell 'em to some rich yanks up

North, huh?"

Captain Hunt tilted his head and squinted at Caleb. "Up North?"

"The Northern States, ring a bell?" Caleb said. "As in not Virginia, Georgia, Alabama, Tennessee, Texas and other great Southern locales?"

"All those States you mentioned belong to Freedonia, sir," the captain replied. "Well, all except Texas; that belongs to New Haiti."

Caleb spun on his heels. His jaw fell slack and his eyes looked as if they would pop out of his head. "What in the Hell? Freedonia? New Haiti? The niggers – hell, can I even *say* nigger now? – the *niggras* done just took over everythang! Boy, I'm hot as a whorehouse on nickel night!"

"Sorry, sir," Captain Hunt said.

Caleb paced back and forth. "I need to infect a few more folks, to relieve some of this stress. Let's turn the crew, the passengers...everybody except these youngsters."

"Are we still going to sell them, sir," Captain Hunt asked. They sell for top dollar in Illinois and Wisconsin."

"Hell no!" Caleb spat. "No more selling the youngins! We *eat* them. Ain't nothin' more tender. Now, let's get to it!"

CHAPTER ELEVEN

The soles of Harriet's feet were on fire. Pine cones and dry twigs bit into her flesh as she sprinted through a dense forest. The full moon cast a silver glow upon the leaves that crackled beneath her heels. The din of hounds barking and growling drew closer. Harriet increased her pace.

She no longer heard the dogs, or the curses of the slave-catchers, so she stopped to rest her weary muscles and catch her breath. *"For a short spell,"* she thought.

"Welcome to my parlor, said the spider to the fly."

Harriet whirled toward the source of the voice, raising a silver carving knife – still sticky with the blood of some unfortunate catcher – chest high.

The most handsome – no, *beautiful* – man Harriet had ever laid eyes upon stepped out of the shadows. The corners of his full lips were spread in an inviting smile. "I'm sorry, did I frighten you?" His husky voice revealed a hint of an English accent.

"You obviously ain't from around here," Harriet said, studying his tall, muscular frame. "You sound like this thang I hunted once, go by the name of Talbot."

"I'm from London, England," the man said. The East End, in the district of Whitechapel. I moved here a while ago. I bought my freedom from...wait...hunted? What did you hunt?"

"Monsters," Harriet replied.

"And now, it appears that *you* are the one who is the prey," the man said.

"Seem so," Harriet said.

The man spread his sinewy arms wide. "Well, you are safe here for the night. The locals are afraid of this forest. They say a terrible beast roams these parts."

"Then, what you doin' out here?" Harriet asked.

"I love the outdoors," the man replied. "Besides, beasts don't frighten me; men do."

"Well, this *wo*-man won't do you no harm," Harriet said. "My name's Harriet, by the way. Harriet Tubman."

"I'm Jake Malloy," the man said, offering his hand.

Harriet took Jake's strong, mahogany hand in hers and shook it. "Pleasure, sir."

Suddenly, Jake's hand became a vice around Harriet's fingers, crushing the dense bones as easily as if he was squeezing an egg in his fist.

Harriet screamed in agony.

Jake threw his head back. A growl escaped his throat. He snapped her head forward, fixing his maddened gaze on Harriet. His beautiful face had been replaced by what Harriet could only describe as the visage of a rabid wolf; a rabid wolf with familiar eyes.

Harriet tried to snatch her pulverized hand out of Jake's grip, but she was too strong and the pain was too great.

Jake yanked Harriet toward him.

Harriet's head snapped back from the

force as her feet skittered across the dirt and dry foliage.

Jake opened his mouth wide, revealing a mouth full of vicious canine teeth. He closed the toothy maw down upon Harriet's shoulder, rending sinew and bone.

Harriet thrust forward with her carving knife, sinking it deep into Jake's chest.

Jake staggered backward, coughing as a crimson cloud of ichor spewed from his mouth.

Harriet collapsed to her knees. Jake fell onto his back, convulsed once; twice; and then, lay still.

Harriet crawled to a large tree and rested her back against it. The pain in her hand and shoulder made it difficult to think; to understand what just happened. Darkness encroached upon her, blurring her vision.

"Still alive, eh?"

Harriet turned her head toward the voice. Jake stood beside her. She turned his gaze toward Jake's beastly form, still lying where he fell.

"How?" Harriet coughed.

She wanted to leap to her feet and run,

but the pain would not allow it.

"What *are* you?"

"What *was* I, you mean," Jake replied. "The thing you hunt."

Jake pointed toward Harriet's wounded shoulder. "Well, hunted. Now, you have the blessing, too."

Tears ran down Harriet's cheeks. "I...I'm gon' turn into a thing like you, now?"

"Maybe," Jake answered. "You become what your spirit is."

"I'm gon' kill you!" Harriet cried.

"You already *have*," Jake said, nodding toward his corpse."

Harriet shut her eyes and succumbed to the darkness.

****

Harriet awakened, naked on cold stone. She sprang to her feet, beating back encroaching nausea and then studied her surroundings. She was still in the sub-basement at the brothel, but it was different. The room was now a wine and rum cellar by the look and smell of it, not a sanctuary for the Spirit-Engine.

Harriet stepped on something soft, wet and cold. She moved her foot and then looked down.

"Oh, no!"

Half of Mary's face stared up at her.

Harriet perused the floor. Bits of Mary were all over it.

Harriet collapsed onto her knees. Her body shook as tears poured down her face. "Mary, you was so hard headed! I could have handled Caleb, myself. The Lawd done showed me he here and he more powerful than ever, but I can kill him. It might cost me my life, but I can kill him, just the same."

Harriet wiped her face with the back of her hand and then stood and walked toward the ladder. "You wasn't 'spose to die here, Mary. You wasn't 'spose to be here at all. You were one of my best friends – a sister, really – a real soldier, sho' 'nuff and one of the best people I ever knowed."

"Aw, I didn't know you loved me so, Harriet!"

Harriet snapped her head toward the source of the voice.

Something like smoke floated before her.

The smoke took on the shape of Mary.

Harriet sucked her teeth. “Cryin’ fo’ the dead and sayin’ good words on they behalf is just the Christian thing to do.”

Mary shook her head. “You cold, Harriet...but you *lyin’*, too. You know you love me. Who *don’t*?”

“Obviously not *you*,” Harriet said, pointing at the mess that was once Mary. “Look what you did to yo’self!”

Mary scratched her phantom head. “Yeah, I’m *all* messed up. We gotta fix that.”

“Ain’t nothin *we* can do,” Harriet said. “Maybe Baas can. The Lawd ain’t let yo’ spirit enter Heaven – or wherever you belong – fo’ a reason.”

“So I ain’t a ghost, cursed to haunt this brothel for all time?”

“Naw.”

“Damn, that would have been kinda fun!”

“Mary! Lawd!” Harriet said, shaking her head. “Well, I reckon I can only sees you ‘cause of my visions the Lawd bless me wit. Let’s find Baas befo’ you waste away altogether.”

Harriet ascended the ladder. She crept through the whorehouse, with Mary's spirit floating behind her.

****

Whitechapel Street was blanketed in shadows. Harriet prayed those shadows would conceal the pink, lace-trimmed skirt and burlesque tailcoat she had stolen from one of the prostitute's chest-of-drawers while she and her paramour slept.

"Over there," Harriet said, pointing toward a shop nestled between a candy shop and a dentist's office. The sign above it read *Telegraph Office.* "I saw somebody in there. Maybe they can give us a clue where we can find this world's Baas."

"Or maybe not," Mary said. "It's awful late for folks to be workin'. And I can sniff things out, bein' a spirit and all."

"Yeah, I know," Harriet sighed. "The Lawd guiding me here, though, so I'm gone follow."

Mary sucked her teeth. "The Lawd? Harriet, you need to stop! You been at this a long time. You *know* something ain't right. You lookin' to get into a scrap, is all."

Harriet strode toward the shop. "Now, why

would I want to do that?"

"'Cause you're wearin' some whore's clothes, lookin' like a lollipop and you ain't heeled."

Harriet frowned. "I loved that *Bello Mule*. Lost that, my goggles, all my stuff."

"Hell, I lost a whole body," Mary said. "What you frettin' 'bout?"

"True," Harriet whispered. "Now, pipe down, I don't want these folks to think I'm talkin' to myself."

Harriet entered the telegraph office. Three men were in the shop. Each sat before a telegraph machine.

"How can we help you ladies?" One of the men asked, looking up from his machine.

Harriet frowned. She took a step back toward the door.

"Oh, don't worry," the man said, smiling. "Negro money spends here."

"That's not my concern," Harriet said.

"What, then?" The man said, rising from his chair.

"Well, considerin' my friend here is a haint

and y'all can see her, y'all must be haints, too." Harriet replied.

The man directed his attention to Mary. "You're a ghost, correct?"

Mary shook her head and then raised her index finger. "A *spirit*."

The two other men stood.

"We're *ghasts*," the man said. "A bit...stronger than our ghost brethren,"

"Hmm...ghasts," Harriet said, studying the trio. "Never had the pleasure of killin' one of you. A friend of mine said you fast and can possess a body for days at a time."

"Who are you?" The man asked. "I, by the way, am Mr. Longshanks. My colleagues are Mr. Brown and Mr. Stein."

Mr. Brown and Mr. Stein nodded.

"Not pleased to meet you," Harriet replied. "I'm Harriet Tubman."

Mr. Longshanks scowled. "Now that's not nice! I have been forthright with you. I expect the same."

"Excuse me?" Harriet said.

"Don't sell me a dog!" Mr. Longshanks

spat. "You lie, you die."

"I ain't lied to you, monster," Harriet said, tilting her head from side to side to stretch her neck. "But, forget all that, let's get to the part where you make me die."

"Harriet Tubman is the Vice President of Freedonia," Mr. Longshanks hissed. "I doubt she would be roaming the streets of Whitechapel at night dressed like a clown."

Harriet smiled. "See, I *was* gonna just walk away, on account of I got somewhere to be. But now, I gots to hurt you."

Mr. Longshanks shook his head. "You can be Vice President, the Queen, hell, even Jesus Christ...we're not taking any beatings in here."

"Oh, you won't have to take it," Harriet replied, raising her fists to her chin. "I'm gon' *give* it to you."

The trio of ghasts exploded forward. Harriet leapt forward to meet them.

The ghasts were quick; frighteningly so. They darted around Harriet, pummeling her with punches, headbutts and knees.

Harriet slumped over a telegraph machine, panting. Blood poured from her mouth and pulverized nose.

Mary swung at the back of Mr. Longshank's head. Her hand went through it as if it was air. "Damn it!"

Mr. Longshanks turned slowly on his heels until he faced Mary. A grin was stretched across his pallid face. "Your fighting days are over, Negress. You cannot help your friend. We have lived in Whitechapel for a thousand years, feeding off the flesh of the downtrodden; possessing the bodies of the well off who hate them so. Now, we will consume your fr..."

A telegraph machine slammed into the top of Mr. Longshanks' skull. The ghast's head disappeared in a crimson cloud.

His headless body collapsed to the floor in a wet heap.

Harriet punched Mr. Stein and Mr. Brown in their chests. Her fists sinking into their torsos up to her wrists. "Y'all fast; I give you that. But your bodies are softer than a velvet bathrobe on a bed of feathers."

The ghasts' eyes rolled back into their heads.

Harriet withdrew her fists.

The ghasts fell to the floor with a loud thud.

Harriet nodded toward Mary. "Thanks for distractin' them while I healed."

Mary returned the nod. "I got your back, as best as I can."

"We gon' get you straightened out, Mary," Harriet said. "I don't know how, but I know we just gotta get to Baas and he gon' figure somethin' out."

"We best get a wiggle on, then," Mary replied.

Harriet walked toward the exit.

"Harriet?" Mary said.

Harriet peered over her shoulder at Mary. "Yeah?"

"Do you think what that ghast said about you bein' Vice President is true?"

"He ain't have no reason to lie. This world *look* the same, but obviously it *ain't* the same. At least we got that clue the Lawd promised me."

"So, we goin' to that...uh...Freedonia place they was talkin' 'bout?"

"I reckon that's as good a place to find Baas as any," Harriet replied. "the Lawd tellin' me he shol' ain't here."

CHAPTER TWELVE

The *SS Savannah* was hailed as one of the most innovative designs in the arena of steamships. The ship was built normally enough, primarily of wood with some metal reinforcements. It was luxurious, with each of the cabins that comprised the Texas deck sporting plush carpets that covered the entire floor and fine quality furniture.

The ship carried forty crew members and up to one hundred passengers. Each of the twenty first class cabins had its own steward while the forty remaining cabins was assigned a steward for every four cabins. The *SS Savannah*'s galley – staffed by two chef's, one from the United States and one from Sicily – was open late to satisfy every culinary whim at whatever hour the passengers desired.

But all these amenities were not what made the *SS Savannah* so unique. The big difference from a more conventional steamship came from the addition of the large windmill-like constructs built all over the top of the ship. Each windmill's vane was connected to elaborate clockwork below decks. When wind struck the vanes, the energy was fed into the iron clockwork, which, in turn, transferred some of its mechanical energy to a series of generating engines that converted the mechanical energy into electrical power.

The electrical power, stored in huge batteries, was used to power the lights, telegraphy and – for a short time, should the ship run out of wood for the steam engine – the ship's propeller.

A strong wind whipped across the deck of the *SS Savannah*, nearly knocking Caleb's crown from his head.

"This wind is a blessing!" Captain Hunt shouted from the pilot house, which sat at the top of the ship, near the bow. "We'll have plenty of energy to recharge our batteries."

"How long before we eat youngin'?" Caleb shouted over the wind. "I'm famished and the galley ain't got nothin' fit for a Ghul King."

Captain Hunt stared at the chronometer on his console. "I had the chefs put the boy on the grill two hours ago. It shouldn't be long now."

"Damn it! I knew a *girl* would be more tinder," Caleb replied. "You will learn to..."

The ship rocked violently as something heavy struck it on the starboard side. Caleb staggered sideways. He stretched his arm to nearly four times its length toward the railing ten feet away. He grabbed the railing, steadying himself.

The ship rocked again.

"What the hell is that?" Caleb shouted. "A wave?"

"No," Captain Hunt said. "The wind is strong, but the water is calm."

"Then, what is it?" Caleb said.

Seemingly in answer, a gargantuan ship rose from beneath the surface of the water less than ten feet from the *SS Savannah*.

"God damn!" Caleb gasped.

"All hands on deck!" Captain Hunt cried into a brass funnel that protruded from his console. His voice sounded throughout the ship.

"A Geobukseon is attacking!"

Caleb craned his head toward the pilot house. "A hot book son? What?"

"A Geobukseon – ka-BOOHK-suhn," Captain Hunt answered. "A Joseon turtle ship."

The Geobukseon was clad in iron plates and the topmost deck featured an iron roof covered in iron spikes. The body of the ship was a combination of wood and iron plates.

Around the sides of the ships several ports opened and cannons protruded from them. On the Geobukseon's main deck, two turrets, built from iron, rose from the deck. Each turret housed a multi-barreled gun that reminded Caleb of a Gatling Gun. The turrets had a wide traverse, allowing it to fire on targets in a 180 to 270-degree arc.

Under the cannons were scores of oars that whirred and clicked as they moved the ship. From the sound, Caleb figured they were powered by machine, not man.

"Joseon…those are Can'ardly people, right?" Caleb asked.

"Can'ardly, your majesty?: Captain Hunt replied, confused.

"As in 'they *can'ardly* see with those

squinty eyes'," Caleb replied. "Orientals, man!"

"Oh. Yes, your majesty."

A panel in each turret on the Geobukseon slid open.

"Get down here, Dick!" Caleb ordered. "Somethin' is happenin'."

The crew and passengers of the SS Savannah – now ghuls in service to Ghul King Caleb – all sprinted onto the deck. Most stopped in their tracks when they saw the turtle ship.

Connor and Colin stood at Caleb's flanks. Captain Hunt stood beside him.

"I believe they are about to board us, your majesty!" Captain Hunt said, his voice trembling.

Caleb turned up his nose and shook his head. He turned toward his subjects. "God damn! In my world, our kind don't fear nothin'. They got half your brain, but ten times your heart. Whatever comes out of that ship is gon' be human. We more than that. *Much* more. So, if them damned Can'ardlies want a fight, then let'er rip! Y'all with me?"

The ship shook from the din of a hundred voices shouting in unison. "Yes, your majesty!"

Out of the open panels in the turrets erupted hundreds of men dressed in the traditional uniform of the elite Hwarang warriors of Joseon: their hair was pulled into a topknot, with a red *manggeon* headband used to keep the hair in place; on their torsos they sported a maroon, blouse, over which they wore a redwood leather vest that held three rockets in their sheaths; on their lower bodies, they wore maroon *baji* – shin-length, baggy trousers – and pointy-toed, red leather *hwa* – boots. Each warrior held a steel sword at the ready as they soared out of the turret, riding wooden sleds powered by large rockets tied to their undersides.

The flying Hwarang cast a shadow over the deck of the *SS Savannah* like a thick cloud heralding a torrential rain. The smell of gunpowder pervaded the air.

"Gather 'round!" Caleb commanded. "These slanty-eyed bastards worship dragons, so let's bring 'em face-to-face with their God!"

The Ghul Army gathered around their king. Caleb guided them to join together; to melt into one another until one's arms became one's legs, became one's torso, and became one's organs.

Within seconds, the army had become

serpentine, forming a giant dragon, with Caleb visage embedded in its massive head. Caleb's crown remained atop the Ghul-Dragon's skull.

The Ghul Dragon coiled and then sprang upward, rushing to meet the descending Hwarang warriors.

The dragon opened its mouth wide.

Scores of Hwarang fell, screaming, into the Ghul Dragon's maw.

The surviving Hwarang landed on the deck of the *SS Savannah.*

Almost in unison, they drew their wooden *seungja-chongtong* hand cannons from the sheaths on their backs and then, with incredible speed, loaded a rocket into them.

The Hwarang fired.

The volley of rockets ripped into the Ghul Dragon's flesh.

A dozen charred ghuls fell to the deck, screaming in agony as they burned away into nothingness.

The Ghul-Dragon turned its gaze at the *SS Savannah.* It opened its mouth wide again and then dived toward the deck.

The Hwarang fired again.

More charred ghuls plummeted toward the deck.

The Ghul-Dragon swallowed the surviving Hwarang.

The ghuls separated into their individual selves. At their feet lie the swallowed Hwarang, writhing and shaking violently.

Caleb held his fist high. “Brothers and sisters…*that* is what victory feels like!”

The ghul army cheered.

“Now, let us prepare to welcome these new soldiers into our ranks,” Caleb said, waving his hands over the infected Hwarang. “Soldiers, I present to you…*the Can’ardly Division*!”

The ghul army roared.

Caleb grinned. He was sure that soon, this world would be his.

CHAPTER THIRTEEN

Harriet combed the docks for hours, searching for a steamship pilot, or even a sailing ship pilot, who could transport her to this strange place called Freedonia.

"No ship from Freedonia has been here in over a year," the Dock Captain grunted, waving his cigar about with pudgy fingers. "The *SS Savannah* left about two hours ago. It was headed to the United States, that's close enough, but I doubt he would have given *you* passage on his ship."

"Yeah, yeah...because I'm a negro," Harriet said with a smirk. "I know."

"Mayhaps," the Dock Captain said. "But more likely because the United States and

Freedonia ain't friends. Your people have gotten awfully toffee-nosed since Freedonia took the egg in your little war and the white world don't like it."

"Good thing the white world is getting' smaller day-by-day, then," Harriet replied.

The Dock Captain grunted, rammed his cigar between his thin lips and then walked away.

"We aren't all barbarians."

The voice came from Harriet's left flank. She whirled toward it, her hand instinctively creeping toward her waist, where the *Bello Mule* would have been. Standing before her was a young man in his early 20s. He was heavily built and massive. On his corpulent shoulders was perched a head with a pronounced brow, alert, steel-grey, deep-set eyes and firm lips, all forming a face that at once expressed brilliance, a hint of arrogance and maybe more than a little laziness.

"Hello, Ms. Tubman," he said. "My name is Holmes; *Mycroft* Holmes. Dr. George Washington Carver – Director of Freedonia's Department for Science, Innovation, Technology and Engineering – has enlisted my services on your behalf."

"Is that so?" Harriet said.

"It is, ma'am," Mycroft replied. "Follow me, please."

Harriet did not move. "What does this Dr. Carver have to do with Baas Bello?"

"I have never heard of this Baas Bello, so I cannot say." Mycroft said.

"Take a wild guess," Harriet said.

"I *never* guess," Mycroft replied. "It is a shocking habit, destructive to the logical faculty."

"*I'm* gon' be destructive to yo' logical faculty if you don't give me some proof this ain't a trap," Harriet said, taking a step toward Mycroft.

Mycroft took a step backward, his soft flesh danced upon his frame. "What I *do* know is you come from...elsewhere, evident by the fact that Harriet Tubman is the Vice President of Freedonia, which you are clearly not."

"How you know I ain't?" Harriet asked.

Mycroft's eyes scanned Harriet's pink skirt and burlesque coat.

"Oh," Harriet croaked.

"I also know that Dr. Carver is well aware of your presence," Mycroft said. "Yesterday, your transportation to Freedonia arrived and awaits you farther up the docks."

"Alright, then," Harriet said with a nod. "Let's go."

Harriet followed Mycroft to a huge sailing ship. *Emancipation* was painted, in red letters, on both sides of its aft end.

Harriet shook her head. "It's gon' take two months to get there in this thing. Freedonia must be seein' hard times."

Mycroft snickered. "This ship merely serves as the landing pad for Freedonia's Dragonflies or Grasshoppers on the rare occasion a Freedonian diplomat pays a visit to the Queen. A Dragonfly is your transportation."

"Where is it, then?" Harriet asked.

Mycroft pointed skyward.

Hovering high above them was an airship unlike any Harriet had ever seen. Constructed of steel and brass, the airship had two wings, which protruded from the center of each side of its cigar-shaped frame. At the end of each wing was an engine that drove two large propellers that tilted backward and forward depending on how the airship dipped, whirled or turned. Protruding from the nose of the craft was a Gatling gun and below it, a cannon.

"Lawd," Harriet thought. *"This Dr. Carver fella 'bout smart as Baas!"*

The Dragonfly descended vertically toward the deck of the *Emancipation.* It landed smoothly. Seconds later, the direct vision window lifted with a hum, revealing a ruggedly handsome man with strong features. The man stood up, he was tall, lean and his weathered, brown face told Harriet he had seen his share of war. He wore a brown, long sleeved blouse, tucked into darker brown trousers. Both the shirt and pants were trimmed with red and blue kente cloth. Atop his head was a dark brown leather beret, which matched his shin high boots. The pilot climbed out of the cockpit onto one of the wings. "Greetings! I'm Major Vernon Clark. Just a moment, Ms. Tubman and I'll send the ladder down."

"No need," Harriet said.

She turned to Mycroft and then shook his hand. "Thank you. Maybe the Lawd will let us cross paths again one day."

"I do hope not," Mycroft sighed. "I mean that as no insult. I have no interest in fighting monsters or gallivanting around the globe solving this and that. I am not built for those things, as you can see. Most people blunder around this city and all they see are streets and shops and cars. I suspect that when one walks with you, they see battlefields."

"Amen," Mary said crossing her heart.

Harriet shot her a glance.

"Ms. Tubman, are we ready?"

"Coming right up!" Harriet replied.

Harriet leapt upward, landing on the wing beside Major Clark.

The major's chin fell to his chest. "How?"

"I eat a lot of molasses with my biscuits," Harriet said. "Puts spring in my step."

"Dr. Carver *said* you were special," Major Clark said.

Harriet blushed. "Aw, I wouldn't say I'm all that."

"And you are so lifelike, too," Major Clark said.

Harriet's smile sank. "Excuse me?"

"Oh, I'm sorry," the major said, covering his mouth. "Did you not know that you are an automaton?"

"Dr. Carver told you that, huh?"

"Yes," the major said. "Is that a problem? Hell, do you even know what a 'problem' is?"

"Yeah, I know what a problem is," Harriet replied. "And no, it ain't a problem. In fact, I can't wait to thank Dr. Carver for telling you that. Let's go!"

Major Clark sauntered toward the pilot's seat. He paused and turned to face Harriet. "You ride in the seat behind me. Oh and Dr. Carver packed you some fresh clothes. I'll stand guard on the wing while you change."

"Thank the Lawd!" Harriet said looking skyward. "You do that. I'll be just a minute or two."

Major Clark stood at the end of the wing with his back to Harriet. Harriet snatched the pink clothing off of her body and then tossed the items to the ground. She quickly slipped on the undergarments and then the gold and red kente cloth brushed twill skirt and blouse. Finally she tied up her leather boots and then hopped into her seat.

Mary appeared in the pilot's seat.

"Mary, get out of there," Harriet

whispered.

"What? Ain't enough room in here for me and him?" Mary replied. "I'm a damned spirit, Harriet; I ain't takin' up no space!"

"Just don't seem right, is all," Harriet replied.

Mary sucked her teeth. "Girl, you just mad Major Pretty-Boy gon' be sittin' on *my* lap and not yours."

Mary shook her head. "Lawd!" She then shouted in the Major's direction. "Ready to go."

Major Clark turned around, jogged toward the cockpit and then leapt into his seat. The direct vision window lowered, locking in place with a soft click.

"Strap in," he said. "We'll be in Alabama in about ten hours."

"Alabama? Is that the capital of Freedonia?" Harriet inquired.

"No, ma'am," Major Clark replied. "Atlanta is the capital. We're going to the Tuskegee Institute. Dr. Carver is eager to see you."

"Got anything to chew on?" Harriet asked.

"I have a few of Dr. Carver's delicious

honey peanut butter sandwiches, a few apples and water," Major Clark said. "But, do you eat, or do you simply simulate eating?"

"Give me one of them sandwiches and some water and I'll eat 'em real life-like for you," Harriet replied.

The major handed Harriet a sandwich wrapped in paper and a metal canteen. Harriet devoured the sandwich and then emptied the canteen of water.

"Fascinating!" Major Clark gasped.

"Give me another one of them sandwiches so I can fascinate you some mo'." Harriet said.

Major Clark gave Harriet another sandwich. "Wait until we take off before you eat that one. Here we go!"

The side propellers spun faster and faster. The Dragonfly lifted vertically, rising higher and higher over the *Emancipation.*

Major Clark looked over his shoulder toward Harriet.

"You're going to love this!" He shouted over the thumping propellers.

Harriet smiled. "Yep. We automatons like flyin' almost as much as we like to eat!"

The *Dragonfly* tilted forward and they streaked ahead, disappearing into the mist and clouds.

CHAPTER FOURTEEN

September 22, 1870

The Dragonfly streaked across the sky. The navy blue sky of evening gave way to the blackness of night, which finally submitted to the red sky of the dawn.

Harriet stretched. She had slept most of the journey. She peered out the window, focusing on the earth below. A country of gentle rolling lowlands greeted her. Minutes later, the Dragonfly flew over a rugged section of land with steep mountain-sides, deep narrow coves and valleys, and flat mountain-tops.

“Alabama, huh?” Harriet said. It did not

look any different from the Alabama of her world. She knew the area well – she had freed many enslaved men, women and children from there. “That was quick.”

“Ah, good, you have turned yourself on,” Major Clark said.

Harriet frowned. “What? I ain’t *never* done that in the company of others!”

“Huh?” Major Clark scratched his head. “Oh, no! Not in that way. As a machine, isn’t that impossible? Anyway, I meant you appeared asleep, which I know automatons don’t need, so I figured you shut down to conserve your energy.”

“I knew what you meant,” Harriet sighed.

“Ah, you were joking,” Major Clark said, laughing nervously. “Wait...you can joke? You have a sense of humor?”

“Fascinating, I know,” Harriet said, rolling her eyes.

“This boy ‘bout smart as rat doo-doo,” Mary said.

Harriet snickered.

“We arrive at Tuskegee Institute in under five minutes,” Major Clark said. “Tighten your seatbelt!"

The Dragonfly descended over one of the fields and began circling. Harriet saw three large buildings encircled by massive evergreen trees. The Dragonfly stopped circling and then landed, vertically, on the roof of the largest building. A tall, thin man dressed in a shirt with a blue and white kente cloth bow tie, blue trousers and a white lab coat stood a few yards away from the Dragonfly.

The man waited until the Dragonfly's propellers stilled before approaching the craft.

The window lifted. Major Clark climbed onto the wing and then hopped down to the ground.

Harriet pushed on the window frame, launching herself out of her seat and over the wing. She landed beside Major Clark without making a sound.

Mary floated beside her.

"Major, thank you," the man said. His voice was high-pitched; almost womanly. "You are dismissed."

The Major bowed slightly. "Yes, sir! Have a good day, sir; Ms. Tubman."

"You, too," Harriet said.

"Harriet Tubman," the man in the white lab coat said, smiling. "Baas Bello has told me all about you; how amazing you are. I am Dr. George Washington Carver."

Dr. Carver extended his hand. Harriet shook it.

"I figured," she said. "You the man who got folks thinkin' I'm some kind of machine."

"Apologies for the facade," Dr. Carver replied. "Major Clark is the only one in Freedonia, besides President Douglass and me, who knows of your presence in our reality and only I and President Douglass will ever know of the existence of an alternate world. It would be dangerous if that got out."

"What about the other Harriet?" Harriet asked.

"Oh, no, she can never meet you," Dr. Carver said. "Baas postulated that if a non-immortal was to ever touch his or her alternate self, the results would be catastrophic."

"So, where *is* this world's Baas?" Harriet inquired. "I'm here for his protection. And why do you know so much about all this?"

"Baas and I are very close," Dr. Carver answered. "He has gone into hiding to escape any attempts on hi, or your world's Baas. I will take you to him soon enough."

"Okay," Harriet replied. "I'll give it a day or two."

"So, how is your friend, Stagecoach Mary Fields?"

"She here," Harriet replied, nodding toward Mary.

Dr. Carver's eyes darted from side-to-side. "Here? What happened?"

Mary, bein' Mary leapt through the openin' made by the Spirit-Engine," Harriet replied. "It tore her apart."

"Oh, my word," Dr. Carver gasped.

"Get to the part where Baas fixes me," Mary said.

"We was hopin' to find Baas soon, to see what can be done to help Mary," Harriet said. "She 'fraid she gon' just waste away."

"I assure you that you will not 'waste away'," Dr. Carver shouted.

"Why is he wailin' like a Banshee?" Mary said. "Tell him I said he sounds like a little girl after her fifth cup o' Arbuckles."

Harriet remained straight-faced. “She says she ain’t deaf.”

“Apologies,” Dr. Carver whispered. “Please, follow me. I believe I have a solution for your...condition, Ms. Fields.”

Harriet and Mary followed Dr. Carver through a door on the roof.

Beyond the door was an iron staircase that spiraled four stories down to the main floor. Iron was carefully wrapped around the window sills, doorways, and balustrades; here the forge’s bright orange belly and the hammer had given birth to all manner of curves, angles, lines and spirals.

“Beautiful work,” Harriet said as she descended the stairs.

“Thank you,” Dr. Carver said. “The work of Blacksmiths from New Haiti. A symbol of our friendship.”

“Their work with iron is some of the best I seen,” Harriet said.

“These lines and curves carry more than meets the eye,” Dr. Carver said. “From fire into iron is where those who wrought lines and curves have folded their messages.”

Harriet ran her hands along the cool,

smooth, black metal. "Messages?"

"Adinkra symbols from the Kingdom of Ashanti have been woven into these wrought-iron designs. Symbols that communicate complex messages and complicated concepts."

Harriet followed Dr. Carver onto a landing above the bottom floor. A plain iron wall stood before them. Dr. Carver placed both palms onto the wall. A few seconds later, the wall hummed, then hissed and then a section of the wall slid downward, leaving a portal a few inches narrower than a common doorway.

Dr. Carver walked through the opening. Harriet and Mary followed him.

The iron panel slid back upward, sealing the wall.

Dr. Carver thrust his arms upward, spreading them wide, as if he was holding a huge ball above his head. "Welcome to Tuskegee Institute's Biological Research and Development Laboratory!"

Harriet perused the capacious room. The laboratory was still. Its tall lights burning brightly and silently. Phosphorus blue light bathed the lab's powerful generator. Electric arcs crackled overhead. Vats filled with a gray sludge pulsated, a hint of pink appearing with each beat.

Harriet noticed there was blood in the sink – brown and some scarlet – and she smelled the peculiar scent of carbolic acid, commonly used as an antiseptic.

Something large and humanoid in shape; something scarred, red and bandaged was bound upon a steel gurney.

Harriet had seen much and, while this place was unsettling, it was not evil. She had seen many horrors; the heights of evil. The feel of this place was not that. It was not intrinsically *good*, but not evil, either – it was more a shade of gray; as gray as the sludge in those vats.

Dr. Carver strode across the room to an area with two rows of alabaster bathtubs. They were empty and dry, except for three, which were covered by a sheet of leather. A metal tube ran from the bottom of the tubs into the floor.

Dr. Carver stopped before one of the covered tubs. "Mary...*this* will bring you back to us."

Dr. Carver snatched the cover off of the tub. Floating within the same gray sludge in the vats was a gray, humanoid figure. It was about five feet tall and rail thin. It had rudimentary facial features – a nose with no nostrils; lips with no opening for a mouth; small lumps where eyes and ears should be.

"I present to you…MAHO!"

"What the hell did he call me?" Mary spat. "I *was* a bit fast in my younger days, but I ain't never traded my treasures for no damned coin!"

"Mary don't like you getting' at she was some kinda pipe organ player, or somethin'." Harriet said.

Dr. Carver's brow furrowed. "Pipe organ…? Oh! No, no…I didn't mean…"

He pointed at the humanoid in the tub. "This is MAHO – *MAlleable Humanoid Organism.*"

"Oh," Harriet said.

"He needs to change that name, then," Mary said.

"Mm-hmm," Harriet replied.

"The sludge in those vats over there is a fungus I was introduced to nearly a decade ago in the rainforests of the Mato Grosso State of Brazil," Dr. Carver said. It is the only fungus known to feed on living organisms, including human beings. But what makes this fungus most incredible is that it absorbs consciousness."

"Another monster to kill, sounds like," Harriet said.

"No, this fungus, which I dubbed the Carver Mushroom, is the neurological network of nature – a biological telegraph, if you will," Carver said. "Interlacing mosaics of mycelium infuse habitats with information-sharing membranes. These membranes are aware, react to change, and collectively have the long-term health of the host environment in mind."

"So, they can communicate with each other and they can protect and heal themselves and whatever they eat," Harriet said.

"Yes!" Dr. Carver said, clapping his hands.

"So they can keep on eatin'," Harriet said.

Dr. Carver stared at the floor. "Well...yes,"

Harriet shrugged her shoulders. "Sounds pretty monstrous to me. How is this going to help Mary?"

"The Carver Mushroom stays in constant molecular communication with its environment," Dr. Carver replied. "And then devises diverse enzymatic and chemical responses to overcome any challenges. I grafted the Carver Mushroom with the preserved cells of Freedonian soldiers who had recently fallen in battle and with the cells of the Namaqua chameleon of Central Africa and, after a few trials, MAHO was born."

"And you want to see if it works by putting Mary's spirit into one of them?" Harriet asked.

"Oh, it works," Dr, Carver said. "I have returned fifteen soldiers mortally wounded in battle to their families. The procedure will be simple...MAHO will absorb Mary's consciousness – or spirit, as you call it. Then, it will duplicate her human form."

"Will she lose the power that the Lawd done brushed her with?" Harriet asked.

"No," Dr. Carver replied. "The powers of the Gifted are simply an expression of the consciousness made manifest in the physical world through the physical form. Mary's Gifts will remain."

"Let's get to it, then," Mary said.

"She ready," Harriet said.

Dr. Carver smiled. "Excellent! Mary, enter the tub. You can lie or stand."

Mary stepped into the sludge, her legs straddling the sides of the humanoid form.

"Is she there?" Dr. Carver asked.

Harriet nodded.

"Good," Dr. Carver said. "You will soon feel as if you are being slowly pulled into the form in the tub. Don't fight it. It is simply you becoming one with MAHO. The process will take half a day to complete, so we will leave you now, but will return in the early morning."

"Bye, Mary," Harriet said.

"Bye," Mary replied. Her voice sounded as if five Marys answered at once.

Harriet turned to Dr. Carver. "Where we goin'?"

"To meet President Douglass," Dr. Carver answered as he retraced his steps toward the door.

"He wear that windblown hairdo over here, too?" Harriet asked.

Dr. Carver swallowed hard. "Umm..."

Harriet giggled. "Aw, come on, Baas. You know what I'm talkin' 'bout."

"Excuse me, Ms. Tubman," Dr. Carver said. "You called me Baas. You must really miss him."

"I know what I called you," Harriet said. "I

done spent my life huntin' the unnatural; the outlandish; the strange. *None* of 'em want to get caught and some is pretty good at hidin'. But *you* ain't, Baas. Not from me. I guarantee Mary know, too; she just ain't sayin' nothin'. And when she get that nose of hers back, she gon' know fo' sho'."

"Yes, you are correct," Dr. Carver replied. "I *am* this reality's Baas Bello."

"What happened to the real George Washington Carver, then?" Harriet asked.

"There never was one," Dr. Carver said. "That is why no George Washington Carver exists in your world. When your world's Baas and I discovered that the death of a person coincides with – and even brings about – the death of their alternate, I decided to permanently conceal my identity, as I was not blessed to have the protection of other, more physically powerful, Gifted as your Baas."

Harriet nodded. "And you put your spirit in one of them MAHO things."

"Yes," Dr. Carver said. The first one. Long before Freedonia existed. Long before I discovered how to graft human cells to the cells of other organisms. While the process was successful, my voice is a bit...unique and I cannot reproduce, as the Carver Mushroom –

actually called that because it cleaves the molecules of its host and attaches itself in the space in-between – has no concept of reproduction as humans do it."

"So, you had to add human cells to the mix to make it right," Harriet said.

"Yes," Dr. Carver said. Excellent, Harriet! Your understanding of genetic science is uncanny."

"I understand crazy pretty good," Harriet replied.

"'That you do," Dr. Carver said. "Such brilliance and power needs to be preserved. When the sun sets on your life, I would hope you find me again so that I may transfer your consciousness to a MAHO."

"Thanks, for the offer," Harriet replied. "But I the Lawd made me tougher than most. So when I'm 'bout to die, ain't no doubt in my mind that it's my time."

"Well, the offer will forever stand," Dr. Carver said. "Let us make haste to the roof. I will call Major Clark so that he can give us a lift."

CHAPTER FIFTEEN

The National House was an immense octagonal, white granite mansion, decorated with cupolas and spires and scrolled balconies. It was located on Peachtree Road, the most select street in Atlanta. The mansion loomed three stories above a well-manicured lawn that surrounded all sides of it. On the outer perimeter of the lawn was an iron fence decorated with the same Adinkra symbols Harriet admired back at Tuskegee Institute.

A wide walkway led from the house to the front gate. Standing on either side of the walkway was a Freedonian soldier dressed in an indigo uniform trimmed in red and blue kente cloth. Each soldier was armed with what looked like a shotgun-sized version of a Gatling Gun.

The weapon was attached, by a metal tube, to a small pack the soldiers wore upon their backs. On the right breast of each soldier was his name; on the left breast, various medals and ribbons. The one medal they all sported was the Freedonian Seal – a circular medal of gold engraved with a 7-pointed star inside of a circle, with a circle, vertical bar and stylized 'x' inside of it. Engraved around the star were the words *Freedonia* and *Honor & Grace.*

The Freedonian seal matched a flag that flew a few yards away from the mansion. The Flag bore the colors red, blue, gold and white – the national colors of Freedonia.

Standing at the gate was a tall woman. She looked as if she had run a mile, a tinge of pink under her tawny beige skin. She wore a fitted skirt of black-and-white pin stripes; a white shirt with ruffled sleeves and front, covered by a black, velvet tailcoat; and black, leather ankle-high boots.

"Good morning, Vice President Tubman; Dr. Carver," she said.

"Good morning, Victoria," Dr. Carver replied.

"Mornin'," Harriet said, following Dr. Carver's lead.

"I thought you left for Africa already, Madam Vice President," Victoria said.

"Naw, not yet," Harriet said. "I ain't get a chance to pick up a much needed dossier from the President, but I'll be up in the air and out of your hair in no time."

Harriet followed Dr. Carver up the stone front steps onto the National House's porch, where two more soldiers greeted them.

The soldiers simultaneously slid one hand up, to the wrist, into slots on both sides of the double doors. There was a low *click*. The soldiers removed their hands and then both doors crept open. Harriet and Dr. Carver stepped inside.

A vast foyer, with polished granite floors and pristine, white walls welcomed them. The foyer sat at the foot of a curving, iron staircase that seemed to ascend into the heavens.

Dr. Carver walked down a long highway off of the foyer. Harriet strode behind him.

Strangely, outside of Harriet's and Dr. Carver's footsteps, there was no sound in the house, not even the sounds that houses make – no distant roar of a furnace, or creak of a stairwell; nothing but silence.

"It's quiet as the grave in here," Harriet

whispered.

"That's due to the sound proofing properties I had built into this house," Dr. Carver said. "It involved building a system of double walls where virtually nothing within one wall was allowed to touch anything in the other – a sort of room *within* a room. Insert sound deadening insulation between those walls and...*voila*!"

They reached a set of double doors. A Freedonian soldier stood at the sides of each of them. One of the soldiers spoke into a brass funnel that protruded about a hand's length from the wall beside one of the double door. "Mr. President...Vice President Tubman and Dr. George Washington Carver are here to see you, sir."

"Send them in," a baritone voice replied through the same funnel the soldier spoke into.

"Yes, Mr. President," the soldier said.

The soldiers pulled the doors open.

"Go on in, Madam Vice President; Dr. Carver, sir," the soldier said.

Harriet and Dr. Carver entered the office.

Frederick Douglass rose from his chair and stepped from behind his desk. He approached Harriet slowly, his eyes scanning her.

"Fascinating!" He said.

"That's what everybody keep tellin' me," Harriet replied.

President Douglass shot a glance at Dr. Carver. "She sounds like our Harriet; looks like her, of course. But can she...?"

Dr. Carver nodded. "I believe she can, sir."

Harriet raised an eyebrow. "Can I what?"

President Douglass skipped forward, letting fly a barrage of hard punches.

Harriet weaved and parried the blows.

She crouched low as she countered with a palm strike to Douglass' chest.

The President flew backward. His buttocks skipped across his desk like a stone thrown across the surface of a pond.

He landed in his chair, eyes wide and jaw slack.

Harriet placed a fist on her hip and then tilted her head. "Lawd, Douglass! Have you lost yo' mind?"

"Apologies, Harriet," Douglass replied. "Our Harriet Tubman is a great soldier and an even better spy. She fights well, but she is no match for your skill and certainly not your speed and strength."

"You just like the Douglass from my world," Harriet said. "He thinks he a pugilist, too."

President Douglass laughed. "I'll have you know that, in *this* reality, I was once Heavyweight Champion of the World."

"Oh, you definitely different from my Frederick Douglass, then!" Harriet said. "He a great speaker, though. If he could fight like he can speak, I reckon *our* Douglass would be a champion, too."

"I rather enjoy fisticuffs and wrestling," Douglass said. I enjoy the struggle of it – the struggle of man overcoming another man; the struggle of man overcoming himself. If there is no struggle, there is no progress"

"We negroes should be the most progressive folks in the world, then," Harriet said.

"Indeed," Douglass said with a nod. He pointed toward two chairs that sat on the other side of his desk. "Please, sit."

Harriet and Dr. Carver sat.

"Dr. Carver told you why I am here, I reckon," Harriet said.

President Douglass leaned forward in his chair. "He told me something about a zombie invasion? The Houngan of New Haiti employ zombies as weapons in their arsenal, dropping those terrible creatures upon their enemies from balloons."

President Douglass shivered.

"What's comin' is ghuls, not zombies," Harriet said. "I done killed a few zombies in my day and a few ghuls, too. Ghuls is much worse. About the worse thing I done ever killed and I done killed a lot."

"How many are on their way?" President Douglass asked.

"I don't know," Harriet answered. "But I *do* know they leader. He a man named Caleb; Brushed by the hand of the Lawd – or maybe that other one; yeah, probably him. Anyhow, he done fashioned himself as the King of Ghuls, seein' as he the first of they kind and all, and he got a powerful itch to make more like him. By now, he probably comin' with an army."

"But, you're not absolutely sure?"

Douglass said.

“Have you not been hearing me?” Harriet said. “You’d best take this serious. Caleb is powerful, hate negroes and crazier than an outhouse rat.”

“And you crossed realities to help us?” Douglass asked.

“Naw,” Harriet replied. “I came to warn an old friend, but he ain’t in Freedonia.”

“Why did you reach out to Dr. Carver, then?” President Douglass inquired.

“My friend, Baas Bello, built a machine that allows him to travel between my world and this one,” Harriet replied. “He admired Dr. Carver’s work and always spoke highly of him. When I found out that his enemy, Caleb had used his machine, I figured he was on Baas’ tail, so I used the machine, too and got in contact with Dr. Carver here, ‘cause I was familiar with his name.”

President Douglass scooted in his chair, turning his torso toward Dr. Carver. “Do you know this Baas Bello gentleman?”

“No, I do not, Mr. President,” Dr. Carver lied. “When Ms. Tubman sent word to me, I was shocked, but I ran a series of tests on her at

Tuskegee and, as you can see, her claims are true, so I also believe her warnings about the ghuls should be heeded."

"Well then, will you help us repel these invaders, Ms. Tubman?"

"Repel? Naw. Kill? Yeah. I reckon if I don't, there won't be no Freedonia left."

"I think you underestimate us, General Tubman," President Douglass said.

Harriet shook her head. "Naw, I just know what you up against. Caleb and his army of ghuls wiped out an entire town within a few hours."

Douglass' skin paled. "But *you* defeated him?"

"Naw, an *army* did," Harriet replied. "Well, almost. But I will."

"How?" Douglass asked.

"Caleb powerful," Harriet said. "But I'm more experienced and got more sense. Caleb got his Ghul Army, but I got the Lawd...oh and I also got Black Mary."

"Black Mary?" President Douglass said, scratching his head.

"'Black Mary' Fields," Harriet replied. "Some call her 'Stagecoach'. She 'bout a army all by herself. You'll be makin' her acquaintance in a bit."

President Douglass laid his large, brown hands over Harriet's. "Harriet, the military might of Freedonia is at your disposal."

Harriet smiled. "Then the good Lawd might just bless us to send Caleb on back to Hell once and for all."

CHAPTER SIXTEEN

September 23, 1870

Morning sun flooded the fungi-filled womb that was the tub in which the MAHO gestated.

A figure stirred beneath the surface of the gray-brown muck. The muck parted as Stagecoach Mary sat bolt upright.

Harriet stood beside the tub, smiling. "Mornin', sleepy head."

Mary blinked rapidly, staring at Harriet with a disoriented gaze. She looked, to Harriet, like some new-born creature, opening its eyes in a world that it had never known.

"H-Harriet?" She said.

"That's me," Harriet replied.

"I'm back?"

Harriet nodded.

"I'm back!" Mary said, perusing her own body; pinching her flesh. "I'm me again!"

She covered her bare breasts with her arms. "Where are my duds? It's chilly in here! 'Sides, I can't have Carver walkin' in here and losin' his mind over all this womanhood."

"Carver is waitin' for us in his office," Harriet said. "There's a table behind those vats over there. Your clothes are on it."

"Alright," Mary said. "You can go on; I'll find you."

"Got your senses back, huh?"

"Yep."

"Alright, then," Harriet said, walking away. She paused, looking over her shoulder. "Good to have you back."

"Thank you, kindly," Mary replied. "Good to have me back, too!"

Harriet walked out of the lab and down a hallway painted light blue. There was a single, iron door at the end of the hall. She knocked on it. Dr. Carver opened it.

"Beautiful, isn't she?" Dr. Carver asked.

"Who? Mary?" Harriet said.

"Yes," Dr. Carver said. "The Carver Mushroom's consumption of Mary's consciousness and replication of her body and her essence was perfect."

"She got her nose back and I reckon her other senses," Harriet said. "What about her strength and her toughness?"

"We will have to put those attributes to the test," Dr. Carver said. "When she is ready, of course."

"How 'bout now, then?"

Mary stood in the doorway, dressed in dark brown leather salopettes – bib-and-brace overalls – tucked into calf-high, brown leather boots. Under her salopettes, she wore a black dress shirt, over which she sported a mocha frock coat.

"You *look* strong," Dr. Carver said patting Mary's thick biceps. "We, however, need to test your limits."

"Let's get a wiggle on, then," Mary said.

Dr. Carver faced the wall at the rear of his office. He placed both palms on the wall. Something inside it whirred and clicked. A second later, the wall slid downward, revealing a vast field of manicured grass. A stone path ran the length of the field and several large metal panels dotted the grass.

"This is where I test our weapons and transportation systems," Dr. Carver said.

"Which one is Mary?" Harriet giggled.

Mary shot a glance at Harriet. "Well, I sure as hell ain't no mule, so, I guess that kinda narrows it down a bit, now don't it?"

Dr. Carver cleared his throat. "If you would be so kind, please follow me to the middle of the field."

Dr. Carver walked briskly across the grass. Harriet and Mary followed him. Dr. Carver stopped before one of the panels. He placed his palm on the panel and it slid open.

Dr. Carver bowed deeply, stretching his hands before them and waving them about as if he was conducting some invisible, silent orchestra.

"Harriet; Mary, it is my pleasure to present to you...Stepton!"

It rose from the ground, held aloft on an iron lift, powered by a steam engine several feet below. It was a creature composed entirely of iron. It had the shape of a heavily muscled man who stood eight feet tall. Its fists were two large iron balls. Its feet were great iron blocks a foot thick. Stepton's face reminded Harriet of the visage of a silverback gorilla. Its eyes were two constantly flickering red lights.

"It doesn't look so tough," Mary said. "Why is its moniker 'Stepton'? Because it weighs a ton?"

"He actually weighs *twelve* tons," Dr. Carver replied. We call him Stepton because, if you get in his way, you will get *stepped on.*"

"He?" Harriet said, raising an eyebrow.

"Stepton possesses limited artificial intelligence," Dr. Carver said. "He thinks at the same level as a six year old."

"And as far as getting stepped on..." Mary snickered. "He's big, yeah, but not big enough to step on nobody. I would beat his a..."

Stepton's legs expanded, tripling his height in less than 5 seconds.

"Uh, oh," Mary croaked.

"Lawd!" Harriet said, shaking her head.

"Maybe I *ain't* ready," Mary said. "I feel a bit played out. I probably need to go take a nap for a while."

Stepton struck. His right fist slammed into Mary like a battering ram into a castle door.

Dr. Carver snapped his head over his shoulder. After a moment, he frowned. "Where is Mary? I expected to see her soaring off in the distance, that punch was so powerful."

Harriet nodded toward Stepton. "There she is."

Stepton was bent deeply at the waist, his right arm extended forward as if he was trying to catch himself from falling. Before him, with her fingers burrowed into his iron fist, crumpling it like it was paper, stood Mary.

"Good Goddess!" Dr. Carver gasped.

Harriet snickered.

Stepton's left fist flew out from his wrist. A thick, iron chain unraveled from within his forearm. The wrecking ball sped toward Mary's head.

Still gripping Stepton's right fist, Mary leapt high into the air.

Stepton's left fist hammered into the

earth, beating a crater into the soft dirt.

Mary snapped her arms upward as she descended, yanking Stepton off his feet.

She torqued her hips, turning in the air.

Stepton sailed over her head.

Mary landed with a loud thud. She snapped her arms downward, pulling Stepton's fist toward the ground.

Stepton's back crashed into the ground. The automaton vomited a torrent of bolts, gears and pieces of wire.

Mary released Stepton's fist.

Stepton lay still.

Mary sauntered toward Harriet and Dr. Carver.

Dr. Carver clapped his hands. "Well done!"

Mary shrugged. "I'm back, baby!"

"Come with me," Dr. Carver said. "We need to run some tests."

"Okay," Mary said. "But I tell you right now, Doc, I feel fine. I..."

Mary's eyelids fluttered rapidly.

Harriet waved her hands before Mary's face. "Mary?"

Mary snapped to attention. She brought the fingertips of her right hand to the corner of her eyebrow.

"I, Mary Fields-Adam Swan-Hank Dobbins-Mary Fields, do hereby swear that I will bear true and faithful allegiance to the President – Supreme Commander of the Armed Forces of Freedonia," Mary said, her eyelids flickering faster and faster. "And that I will bear true faith and allegiance to the Government of Freedonia as by law established, and that I will serve in the Armed Forces of Freedonia and go wherever ordered by air, land, or sea and that I will observe and obey all commands of the Government of Freedonia as by law established and of any officer set over me, according to regulations and the Uniform Code of Military Justice. This, I swear before God and the Ancestors."

Harriet snapped her head toward Dr. Carver. "Dr. Carver, what's wrong?"

"As I told you earlier, the Carver Mushrooms share information with each other," Dr. Carver replied. "Normally, when a colony of absorbs a lifeform, they cut off communication with other colonies and communicate exclusively within their community. Mary's incredible level of physical exertion – probably in tandem with her gifts – most likely strained her cells' regulation of the neural network established by the Carver mushrooms. She must be connected to the consciousnesses of the soldiers who are now one with MAHO."

"How do we fix it?" Harriet asked.

"She will probably return to normal once she recovers from the strain of her encounter with Stepton. At any rate, we need to run some tests. I also need to check on the MAHO soldiers. Please, take Mary to the laboratory and return her to her tub. I will return shortly."

Mary, still at attention, did not say anything else, but her eyelids continued to flicker at light speed. Harriet tossed Mary over her shoulder and then jogged to the laboratory.

"Lawd," she said looking skyward. "Protect yo' daughter, Mary. She bear yo' mother's name, so I know you partial to her, Lawd. Caleb will be here soon and I need Mary at my side if we gon' win this thing. Amen!"

CHAPTER SEVENTEEN

September 24, 1870

The world had always been a cruel place for Captain Barnabus Sneed. His scars were many and deep. Growing up, his teachers and parents had labeled him a problem child, emotionally disturbed and even, at one point, a lunatic.

Wanting desperately to fit in somewhere, young Barnabus volunteered for the United States Navy. The military taught Captain Sneed how to pour the burdens of his soul into the killing of other men - Black men, especially. With each death of a Freedonian or New Haitian he wreaked in the Reunion War on behalf of God and country, he peeled back a layer of scar tissue and felt a sense of hope that he might one day become a man others could respect, if not love, maybe even a man who could learn to love himself.

Now, he was a Captain in charge of securing New York Harbor.

Tonight was a special night. Every full moon, in a tradition he had started during the Reunion War, Captain Sneed did two things: First, he tossed fresh flowers into the Atlantic Ocean in honor of his fallen comrades. Then he read his latest poems to the waters and the winds.

Writing poetry helped him deal with all his pent-up emotions. It had helped him through his roughest times: the loss of his dog, Jessup – his only friend – when he was nine, all the hell he had gone through in the New Jersey State Lunatic Asylum and the rocky period that followed when he turned sixteen and ventured out on his own.

Captain Sneed sat in his steam-powered carriage, gazing at the water, eager to share his work with the Seamen who had fought so bravely at his side. As he climbed out of his car, he noticed a large ripples upon the surface of the ocean.

“The fish have come to honor you, too, my brothers,” he said.

This quiet spot, on the farthest end of the dock, was always empty. The Seamen under his charge knew that this was 'Captain Sneed's Spot'. He patrolled it; he secured it. And no one questioned it. Captain Sneed, after all, enjoyed killing and many a Seaman believed his enjoyment didn't just stop at killing Freedonians and New Haitians.

Captain Sneed called this spot "Realm of the Fallen."

His father had actually taken him here once – long before the New Jersey State Lunatic Asylum; long before the Reunion War – because the fishing was good. He taught Captain Sneed how to work a rod and reel, gut a fish with a knife, skin it and flay it. Captain Sneed was good with a blade and took a secret delight in gutting fish. That was the best day of Captain Sneed's childhood, before the New Jersey State Lunatic Asylum.

Captain Sneed walked to the water's edge with his journal. The moon's glow cast his shadow across the ocean's glassy surface.

"Greetings, my brothers!" He said. "I have some new poems for you."

He opened his journal, feeling the worn leather cover against his palms. The oversized book, filled with hundreds of pages of his handwriting and drawings, was a memoir of his inner world from childhood to now. The stiff, heavily inked pages crinkled as he turned them, and that sound always made him feel a sense of nostalgia.

The book had been a gift from his mother on his ninth birthday – one of his parents' attempts to see where their child fit in; to make him like other "normal" children. Across these pages he had written countless poems and short stories and had drawn things he wanted to one day own or become.

The last fifty-five pages were filled with his love poems, some so sappy he felt embarrassed to read them. Most of his poems were musings, amateurish and base, but every now and then he wrote something he was proud of. The only ones who had ever heard any of his writings were Jessup, his fallen comrades and the ocean.

Captain Sneed held the big book open like a preacher about to give a sermon, only his congregation was the fish and the reeds and the dark water.

"I've been seeing Jennifer around the docks more and more. Today she gave me a gift and kissed me on the cheek. The way she acts around me sometimes, I...I think I might actually have a shot with her."

He felt his heart expand just thinking about her. He blushed as he read on.

"Her beauty has awakened something in me that I have never felt for anyone. I cannot stop writing about her. I have written at least a dozen new

poems. They are all about her. This first one is still a work in progress. The beats are not quite right, but this is what I have written thus far."

He read the poem aloud:

"Her eyes? Fireflies.

Flames in her caress,

We embrace, we smile,

Cannons in our chests.

Time's first gentle touch,

Feathers along our flesh.

Nobody is around us,

We whisper, touch, undress.

Butterflies in our minds,

Spreading wings together.

Taking flight in purple skies,

Evaporating like hot weather."

The sound of hands clapping startled Captain Sneed.

"That is the most beautiful piece of shut-the-hell-up I ever heard," a man's voice echoed off the water, followed by laughter.

Captain Sneed turned to see Caleb, standing several yards away.

"Who in the hell are you?" Captain Sneed spat, drawing his cutlass from the scabbard that bounced on his thigh.

"You? You mean *'we'*?"

Caleb nodded toward something behind Captain Sneed.

The Captain turned back toward the ocean. Before him, in the moonlit ocean, loomed the *Geobukseon.*

****

On the docks, the ocean watched in silence as Captain Sneed crawled across the boardwalk, dragging his wounded legs. A withered ghul's finger, separated from its owner, jutted from the back of one thigh. Moonlight glinted off the exposed bone of Captain Sneed's hip. Hair, caked with blood and dirt, clung to his face as he clawed his way toward the water. He spotted one of the Seamen under his command, or what was left of him, floating face down near the shore. Hugging his butchered torso, Captain Sneed wailed, an animal cry that echoed across the ocean.

A flock of ducks, startled out of there slumber, took flight, quacking in protest.

Behind Captain Sneed stood Caleb. Then Colin and Connor joined appeared, their clothes covered in dark stains. The Ghul King and the twins sauntered up the boardwalk toward the Captain.

Captain Sneed rolled off the boardwalk, landing in the mud near the shore. He struggled onto all fours and then scrambled toward the water. Upon reaching the shore, Sneed dove into the ocean. He attempted to swim away, flailing his arms, but Connor and Colin waded in after him and brought him screaming back to shore. Caleb resumed torturing the man, breaking off another finger and then stabbing it into the side of Captain Sneed's shoulder.

Captain Sneed whimpered; he no longer had the strength to scream. Besides, his men were dead; there was no one to help him.

"Who can help me get into Freedonia?"

"I told you...no one can," Captain Sneed replied. "Not without breaking the truce of

1866."

"Oh well," Caleb said with a shrug. "I guess after I finish you off, I'll find that Sweet little Jennifer you were goin' on about in that little ditty of yours."

"W-wait!" Captain Sneed cried. "There is one man who might be able to get you into Freedonia.

"Who might that be?" Caleb asked.

"Jeremiah Hamilton," Captain Sneed replied. "They call him the 'Prince of Darkness'."

"And what makes you think he can get us into Freedonia?" Caleb said.

"Because he's rich, powerful," Captain Sneed said. "And a Negro."

"Wait…this Hamilton fella is a smoke?" Caleb chuckled. "More like the Prince of Darkies, I reckon."

Connor and Colin laughed.

Caleb squatted down beside Captain Sneed. "Well, since you were kind enough to give us the name of this smoke, Hamilton, who just might be our ticket into Darky Town, we won't hurt your beloved Jennifer…"

"Thank you," Captain Sneed sighed.

Caleb stood and then pressed the heel of his boot into Captain Sneed's jaw. "But you? Oh, we gon' hurt you enough for the both of y'all!"

At dawn, Captain Sneed's screams finally ended. The ocean watched in silence as Caleb and the twins pranced around his corpse. The rest of the Ghul Army swarmed out of the turtle ship and joined their King in the macabre dance under the light of the full moon.

CHAPTER EIGHTEEN

September 25, 1870

For as many years as anyone in the city could remember, Jeremiah G. Hamilton had been a broker of Wall Street. Every morning, his steam-powered carriage could be seen putt-putting from his mansion in Brooklyn, down past the street vendors with their apples and cheese, standing ankle-deep in horse manure and onward to 18 Broad Street, between the corners of Wall Street and Exchange Place, in the Financial District of lower Manhattan.

Some mornings, Hamilton – the only Black millionaire in New York – would pause at the tobacconist's or the newsstand before entering the hallowed halls of the New York Stock Exchange.

From that moment until the lunch hour and again from one o'clock until six, Hamilton lived and breathed the exchange of foreign currencies. Under his adept hands, dollars became pounds sterling; rubles became marks; pesos, kroner; yen, francs. Whatever exotic combination was called for, Hamilton arranged with a smile, a kind word and a question about the countries which minted the currencies he passed under the barred window. Over years, he had built nations in his mind; continents. Every country that existed, he could name, along with its particular flavor of money, its great sights and monuments, its national cuisine.

On Wall Street, he was cleverer and more ruthless than most of his white peers. But as soon as Hamilton left his Wall Street office, he was not even a second-class citizen and subject to the racism that held sway on the streets.

At the deep brass call of the closing gong, he pulled the shutters closed again. From six until seven o'clock, he reconciled the books, filled out his reports, wiped his slate board clean with a wet rag, made certain he had chalk for the next day, drew his Colt 1848 Baby Dragoon Pistol from a pocket inside his satchel and slipped it into his waistcoat. He then stepped lively to his awaiting carriage, climbed in and sat back, formulating more strategies for making money, as his driver transported him home.

Hamilton's estate was reputed to rival the Astor's. His servants were numberless as ants; his personal fortune greater than some smaller nations. And New York feared him.

After the devastating Great Fire of 1835 in New York, Hamilton profited handsomely, taking pitiless advantage of several of the fire victims' misfortunes to pocket some 5 million dollars. Had the authorities of New York known that it was Hamilton who started the fire, they would have hung him. But they had no clue; only his wife, Eliza and Hamilton, himself, knew. And neither of them was telling.

There was no way for anyone besides Hamilton himself to know which of the thousand stories and accusations that accumulated around him were true. There was no doubt that violence and sensuality and excess were the stuff of which his life was made. If his wealth, wits and a web of blackmail and extortion had not protected him, he would no doubt have been dead years before.

The steam-powered carriage sped toward the tall iron gate that surrounded Hamilton's mansion. The gate's double doors opened and the carriage continued up the road leading to the back of Hamilton's home. The vehicle pulled into the garage. Hamilton hopped out when it came to a stop. The engine sputtered, coughed and then fell silent.

Hamilton turned toward a hand-carved door of ivory at the rear of the garage. The door opened. Hamilton's butler held its brass doorknob.

"Good evening, sir," the butler said, his British accent not fully concealing his Fijian one.

"Good evening, Rasolo," Hamilton said. "How are you?"

"Just dandy, sir," Rasolo replied. "We have guests, sir."

"Who?" Hamilton whispered. "How many?"

"Five, sir," Rasolo said. "They are unfamiliar, sir."

"Associates of Eliza?"

"No, sir."

"Then, why in the hell are they in my house?"

"They were quite...insistent, sir."

Hamilton drew his Baby Dragoon.

Rasolo placed a firm hand upon

Hamilton's forearm.

Hamilton glared at him.

Rasolo shook his head.

Hamilton slid the revolver back into his waistcoat. He then strutted down the hall and into his parlor.

Caleb, Connor, Colin, Captain Hunt and one of the Joseon Hwarang Warriors – a stocky man dressed in a uniform similar to his comrades, but colored pristine white – and Hamilton's wife, Eliza, occupied the room. They sat in plush leather chairs and on a leather couch. Eliza sat beside Caleb, who grinned as Hamilton entered the parlor.

Eliza leapt from the couch, walked briskly to her husband and embraced him.

"Hello, dear," she said. "These men have come to discuss a pressing matter with you. I would like to introduce you to Caleb Butler...umm..."

She glanced at Caleb. Caleb nodded. She continued. "King."

Hamilton shifted his attention to Caleb.

Caleb rose and held his hand out toward Hamilton. Hamilton shook it.

"Might I ask, king of where?" Hamilton said.

"*Every*where," Caleb replied.

Goosebumps erupted all over Hamilton's flesh. He tried to snatch his hand out of Caleb's grip, but the Ghul King held on, tightening his grip.

Caleb pulled Hamilton close and then wrapped his arm over Hamilton's shoulders.

"But where are my manners?" Caleb said. "Let me introduce my council: the twin giants over there are Connor and Colin..."

The twins nodded.

Caleb pointed toward the Hwarang warrior. The warrior stood. "And my slanty-eyed camarado goes by the moniker Kim Kang-min, Taejwa, or Colonel, but I like the sound of Taejwa better, of the Joseon Navy."

Colonel Kim bowed slightly.

"Did I get them names right, Kang-min?"

"You did, Your Majesty," Colonel Kim replied.

"Kang-min is our interpreter," Caleb said. "He speaks nine languages."

"Riveting," Hamilton said dryly. "Why are you in my home again?"

"A right down to business kind of fella, huh?" Caleb said. "Usually, you smokes like to beat the devil 'round the stump. I reckon 'cause of havin' to work, all speedy-like, from sun up to sun down, for free for hundreds of years and all."

Hamilton pushed Caleb away and then drew his revolver.

Caleb laughed. "Come on, now, Prince of Darkies. Shootin' me will just get you and your wife killed - her first, so you can watch - and your house burned to the ground. But hear me out and we all end up happy."

Hamilton aimed the revolver at Caleb's brow. "I don't fear death. My only fear is that I'll be reincarnated as a white man. For my wife's sake, however, I will give you two minutes to explain."

"Fair enough," Caleb said. "Look, I need to get into Freedonia, but I and my army are not of the right hue to blend in. But you have the ways, means and color to waltz into Freedonia without anybody battin' an eye."

"I have plans for a railroad that will run through Freedonia and New Haiti," Hamilton said. "I do not wish to see the country destroyed."

"Who said anything about destroyin'?" Caleb said.

"You mentioned an army," Hamilton replied.

"I'm huntin' someone," Caleb said. "The army is for them, *not* Freedonia."

Hamilton's brow furrowed. He shook his head. "An army for one person?"

"For this person, an army is necessary," Caleb replied. "Now, we could sweeten the pot if you agree to help me. Why negotiate with Freedonia when you can rule it?"

Hamilton snickered. "I see...you're mad. You can't..."

"You rule Freedonia," Caleb said, interrupting him. "And I rule the United States."

"Impossible!" Hamilton hissed.

Caleb rolled his eyes. "Show him."

He extended his arms. Connor thrust his head into one of Caleb's armpits. Colin thrust his head into the other. The men's head's disappeared and then their bodies melted into

Caleb's, doubling his size. Colonel Kim drew his sword and then thrust it into the back of Caleb's left arm as he melded into Caleb's back. The Ghul King grew two more feet in height. His left hand was replaced by a razor sharp blade of flesh.

Caleb grinned. "My army and I fit together like pieces in a puzzle. A puzzle whose shape is only limited by our imagination."

Hamilton staggered backward. He slumped down into a chair, breathing heavily. His hands shook, but he never took the muzzle of his revolver off of Caleb. "You...you're all duppy!"

"Duppy?" Caleb said, scratching his head with the blade. "Dead puppy?"

"A malevolent spirit," Hamilton said.

"I guess we are duppies, then," Caleb said with a shrug. "We prefer ghul, though. I got that name from a book I read when I was just a little pup...umm...*dup*."

"William Beckford's 1786 novel, *Vathek*," Hamilton said.

Caleb's eyes widened. "That's the one! You are full of surprises!"

"You are, too," Hamilton replied.

"Yes, our ghul transformations can be quite startlin'," Caleb said.

"You misunderstand," Hamilton said. "I am surprised that such a redneck as you can read."

Caleb laughed. "You are game as a banty rooster! A smoke with your audacity is scarce as hen's teeth."

"How did you become King of these...ghuls?" Hamilton asked.

"I am the first," Caleb replied. "The most powerful. When another ghul is made – by scratch or bite – they instinctively know who their king is."

Hamilton lowered his Baby Dragoon. "I will get you into Freedonia only if you do something for me first."

"Name it," Caleb said.

"I have a rival – an enemy, really, who wrested from my grasp control of the *Accessory Transit Company*, an enterprise that ran a steamship line from New York to San Francisco through Nicaragua."

"His name?" Caleb asked.

"Cornelius Vanderbilt," Hamilton replied.

"You want him dead?" Caleb said.

Hamilton shook his head. "Worse...I want him to serve me. And I want him to transfer every penny of his wealth into Eliza's bank accounts."

"Done," Caleb said. "Just tell me where to find this Cornelius Vanderbilt fella and I'll deliver him to you – and his money to your wife's bank – before high noon tomorrow."

"Excellent," Hamilton said. "Bring your army with you tomorrow and we will leave immediately."

A din like a heavy hail storm beat upon Hamilton's roof.

Caleb pointed toward the ceiling. "No need to bring them. They are already here."

CHAPTER NINETEEN

Mary was a colony. A settlement. A new but flourishing culture. She had the appearance of a woman – the mind, nerves and feel of a woman too. All the normal parts and equipment. But, in her mind, she now existed primarily as a locale, not a woman.

"Mary...are you *you*?"

Black Mary opened her eyes. Harriet sat at her bedside. Dr. Carver stood behind her.

"I'm me," Mary said. "Hopefully for good, right Doc?"

"I was able to break the connection through some advanced neuro-hypnotism techniques I learned during an extended visit among the Nuba," Dr. Carver said.

"Hypnosis?" Mary inquired. "That's another word for mesmerism, ain't it?"

"Nubian hypnosis is much older than mesmerism and approaches the science differently," Dr. Carver said. "Instead of placing direct suggestions or commands into your subconscious mind while you are in a relaxed state, the Nuba use metaphors to get the desired result. Mary, your subconscious mind instantly made the connection between the metaphors and the desired behavior while the metaphor itself acted as a distraction to the Carver Mushroom, which is unable to comprehend metaphor. Thus, the Carver Mushroom broke its connection as it attempted to understand the metaphors."

"Those damned mushrooms see me as some type of...land," Mary said, shivering a bit.

"What makes you say that?" Harriet asked.

"They told me," Mary answered. "They said *'Mary! Oh, Land of Mary. Do you hear us, oh Maryland? Do you hear us?'*"

"Fascinating!" Dr. Carver gasped. "They speak to you? It must be due to your gifts. I have never experience anything like what you are going through."

"I didn't actually *hear* them with my ears, you understand?" Mary replied. "It wasn't a voice. It was all thoughts inside my noggin. But, to me, they came as a thousand voices, talkin' all at once."

"Lawd," Harriet said.

"And nobody else whose spirit has been put in MAHO has gone through what I am?" Mary said.

"No," Dr. Carver replied. "Your experience is absolutely unique."

"Of all the people in the world, why me? Why did I have to be picked to be a territory?"

"I would posit they view us all that way," Dr. Carver replied. "You are just the only one lucky enough to be able to communicate with them."

"So, how long before they link me up to all the other Carver Mushrooms again?" Mary asked.

"You should not experience any issues as long as you do not exert yourself too much," Dr. Carver said.

"Fightin' men and monsters is what I do, Doc," Mary said. "How am I gonna do that without sweatin' up a storm?"

"Perhaps it is time to hang up your guns and do something else," Dr. Carver replied. "I am in need of a courier. I believe you are the perfect candidate."

"If I was a preacher in Paradise, I still wouldn't hang up my guns," Mary said.

"Well, I will make allowances for your guns if you agree to work for me," Dr. Carver said.

"I might consider that if I wasn't going home after we end Caleb," Mary said.

Dr. Carver stared down at the floor. Harriet looked away.

Mary's eyes darted back and forth, between Harriet and Dr. Carver. "Harriet? Doc?"

"The MAHO can't survive the trip through the Spirit-Engine," Harriet croaked.

"What?" Mary said, sitting bolt upright. "You mean to tell me I'm stuck in this world forever?"

"Yeah, Mary, you are," Harriet replied.

"In your world, the Carver Mushroom does not exist," Dr. Carver said. "So, unfortunately, the MAHO cannot be created by the Baas Bello of your reality."

"Give me a minute," Mary sighed.

"Mary..." Dr. Carver began.

"Give me a goddamned minute!" Mary shouted, leaping from the bed.

Harriet grabbed Dr. Carver's arm and pulled him away. "Let's go. Mary, meet us in Dr. Carver's office when you ready. We gotta get heeled."

Mary nodded.

Harriet and Dr. Carver walked away, leaving Mary alone with her tears.

****

Harriet followed Dr. Carver to his office.

"Would you like a peanut butter and honey sandwich and some apple cider?" Dr. Carver asked, opening his icebox.

"Yes, sir," Harriet replied. "You know I'm partial to them sandwiches."

Dr. Carver picked up a beer mug that sat on his desk. He pressed the lever on the pewter lid with his thumb and the lid flew open. Dr. Carver poured cider from a quart bottle and then slid the bottle back into the icebox. He handed the mug and a sandwich wrapped in paper to

Harriet.

"Thank you, kindly," Harriet said.

"It is my pleasure," Dr. Carver said. "For now, it is still a delicacy, but soon, I will have my peanut butter in every store in Freedonia."

"Give me the recipe to take back to Baas," Harriet said. "We'll put it in the stores there, too and I'll spend the rest of my days a rich woman."

"I certainly will," Dr. Carver said.

"So, where are the weapons?" Harriet asked. "I feel naked as Adam and Eve without 'em."

"They are in this cabinet," Dr. Carver said, patting a brass-trimmed, pine cupboard. "My staff has worked night and day to create replicas of your weapons, based on your specifications. I will leave you – and Mary, when she decides to join you – to it. I have to go to the National House and activate the four Steptons I had shipped there last night."

"Mary and me will be in Atlanta directly," Harriet said. "After we done tested these weapons real thorough."

"Until, again, we meet."Dr. Carver bowed and exited the room.

****

The weapons slid on one by one – two Carver Dragoon revolvers and the Carver repeating rifle. Mary surveyed herself in the mirror, gave a thin little smile of satisfaction, and headed for the door.

"Lawd," Harriet said, shaking her head. "You 'bout the only one I ever known who gets comfort from a gun. Glad you feelin' better, though."

"Never underestimate how much assistance, how much satisfaction, how much comfort, how much soul and spirit there is in a six shooter and a well-made carbine," Mary said.

Harriet chuckled. "You sound like you talkin' 'bout a man you fancy."

Mary broke into song, holding her carbine high, as she strutted out the door. "All I need in this life of sin is me and my boyfriend..."

Harriet shook her head.

Now, finally alone in the office, she laid her weapons before her, checking over them with a skill honed to a razor's edge by decades of war.

She unloaded and cleaned the *Carver Mule*. After double-checking that the revolver was purged of oil, dirt and gunpowder, she tested its hammer, trigger, and firing pin. Satisfied the *Mule* was in perfect working order, she loaded it.

Harriet then strapped a scabbard to her waist, letting it hang down her left thigh. She inspected her spadroon, checking the sword's keen, iron edge. It was more beautiful than the spadroon she wielded in her reality, with a multi-ridged ivory grip and a brass hilt replete with a five-ball counter guard and knuckle bow. She slid the sword into the scabbard, and holstered the *Carver Mule* in a pouch she wore across her chest.

"Lawd, I'm grateful to you and Dr. Carver for the weapons," Harriet said, gazing at the ceiling. "I promise to kill plenty ghuls in yo' name, Lawd; an' anything else you might see fit for me to kill along the way."

CHAPTER TWENTY

Hamilton and Eliza stood on the guest house's full front porch.

Caleb perused the house. It had a high gabled roof, the ridge of which was parallel to the walkway that ran in front of the Creole cottage, accommodating the porch as well as the mass of the house.

Two glass doors on the porch led to rooms within the house. An ebony door, trimmed in brass, was positioned at the center of the porch, behind Hamilton.

The guest house rose, basement and all, from its foundation upon ten iron, spider-like legs – five legs on each side of the house.

The house lumbered onto the walkway and then the legs retracted into the house. A series of massive tracks – highly tooled steel plates, linked together in a loop and placed around iron wheels – replaced them. Each track was set upon long axles that were free to swivel around a common axis. This arrangement gave the house maximum adaptability to the contours of the ground. It crept, moving level along the ground, with one "foot" high upon a hillock and another deep in a depression, holding itself erect and steady even upon a steep hillside.

Immense iron plates unfolded from the roof, covering the exterior of the house.

"Damn, Hamilton," Caleb shouted. "Looks like this house could stop an attack from an army of Gatling Guns!"

Hamilton smirked and shook his head. "Oh, the house is much more adamantine than that. The plates are quite thick and can withstand the blasts of several large artillery rounds."

"You expectin' war to come your way sometime soon?" Caleb said.

"I'm a Negro man with a white wife," Hamilton said. "War is always imminent."

The porch's steps flattened and then extended outward, forming a bridge.

"Come on up," Hamilton said.

"You have enough room for all of us?" Caleb inquired.

"The basement can accommodate 200 people comfortably," Hamilton replied. "There is more than enough room."

Caleb looked over his shoulder at the army of ghuls, who stood in columns behind him. "Let's go!"

Colonel Kim repeated Caleb's order in the common tongue of Joseon. "Gaja!"

"Council on the main floor," Caleb barked. "The rest of you, in the basement."

"Mein cheung-e wiwonhoe," Colonel Kim shouted, translating Caleb's orders. "Dangsin ui nameojineun, jiha lo idong."

The army of British, American and Joseon ghuls flowed into the house like a blue and red river, overflowing from a heavy spring rain. Caleb joined Hamilton and Eliza on the porch.

"Who's driving this monstrosity?" Caleb asked.

"My wife and four men under my employ," Hamilton answered.

“Speaking of which,” Eliza said. “I had better head up to the Command Bridge and get this thing moving.”

“Have some absinthe to relax your nerves first, my love,” Hamilton said. “Oh, Cornelius!”

A ghul skittered out of the house. The creature was dressed in a cream-colored tuxedo with matching gloves and chestnut leather shoes. If anyone had seen the ghul about town anywhere in New York City, they would have recognized poor Cornelius Vanderbilt, once one of the most powerful men in the world, now the servant of his rival, Jeremiah G. Hamilton.

“Yes, sir?” Cornelius said.

“Bring three glasses of absinthe,” Hamilton replied.

“Yes, sir,” Cornelius said.

“Hurry, Cornelius,” Hamilton said. “If you take longer than five minutes, I will make you gnaw off one of your toes.”

“Yes, sir,” Cornelius repeated before skittering off.

“That’s cold,” Caleb said, shaking his head.

“That is the best way to serve the dish

called *revenge*," Hamilton replied.

Cornelius returned with a tray upon which sat three crystal stemmed glasses filled halfway with verte absinthe. Hamilton, Caleb and Eliza took a glass and sipped the strong, green spirit, while Cornelius stood in the doorway, awaiting his next command.

"Enjoy," Hamilton said. "Relax in the parlor, study, or dining room. We leave in five minutes and should arrive in Freedonia by tomorrow night."

"So, the house is well-armored," Caleb said, taking a sip from his glass. "But what about its offenses? If things get ugly at the border of Freedonia..."

"I assure you, they won't," Hamilton said. "But to answer your question, the *Ann Eliza Jane* – I named the house after my beloved wife, for, like her, it is powerful, yet brings me much comfort – is armed with four Gatling Guns that extend out of slots on each side of the house's bottom floor and a fifth on the roof in case we are attacked from the air."

"Sounds like you thought of most situations," Caleb said. "Except for where I and my Council sleep."

"There are nine bedrooms in this house,"

Hamilton replied. “The Master Bedroom belongs to Eliza and me. You and your...men may occupy the rest. There is also plenty of food and water. Should any of your soldiers need to exit the house for any reason, there is a door hidden in the floor of the basement they can sneak out of, or they can use either of these doors when the house is not in motion. Once we get going, though, the exterior of all doors and windows will be covered by metal plates and electrified.”

Caleb took another sip of absinthe. “Bully for you, Hamilton. I’m gonna go inside and address my Council.”

“After I escort my wife to the Command Bridge, I will join you,” Hamilton said.

Caleb entered the house and walked to the parlor, where his Council of Colin, Connor and Colonel Kim awaited him. The Council snapped to attention. Caleb waved his hands in a downward motion.

“Sit; sit,” he said. “I want you to relax. There will be plenty to do once we arrive in Freedonia.”

The men sat down on the couch. Caleb sat in a chair, facing them. He leaned forward in his seat before he spoke again.

“Once we take Freedonia, I’m gonna kill

that uppity smoke," he whispered. "Then, I'm gonna turn his wife and her crew and this house will be my palace."

"Do me and me brother still get to rule England?" Connor asked.

"Serve me well and you get to rule all of *Europe*," Caleb replied. "Kang-min, I'll still need you by my side as my interpreter, but you can have all of Asia...except India. India is white man's country."

"Yes, Majesty," Kim said, with a slight bow.

"In just a few days, the age of man comes to an end," Caleb said. "No more playin' around."

"We're gonna be gods," Colin chuckled. "And I'm gonna be naughty! I'm gonna be a naughty Ghul God!"

The parlor erupted into laughter as the *Ann Eliza Jane* rolled onward toward Freedonia.

CHAPTER TWENTY-ONE

September 27, 1870

Jeremiah Hamilton rode next to Eliza in the Command Bridge, perusing the landscape of Maryland. The Appalachian Mountains rose out of the mist to the West. A movement caught his eye. He held a hand high and the *Ann Eliza Jane* ground to a halt.

A moment later, the din of running feet came from the hallway outside of the Command Bridge.

Caleb burst into the room. “What’s the skinny, Hamilton?”

Hamilton pointed to the east. They were in the vicinity of where the Potomac River flowed into the Atlantic Ocean.

"We are at the boundary between Maryland and Virginia," Hamilton said. The border between the United States and Freedonia."

"Good!" Caleb said, clapping his hands.

Hamilton pointed toward the observation window in the ceiling.

Caleb stared up into the sky in the direction Hamilton pointed and his face went wan.

"What is it?" Caleb said, squinting at an object in the distance that zoomed toward the house.

"Aircraft," Hamilton growled.

"Ain't like no airship I ever seen," Caleb said.

"The Freedonians call it a Dragonfly," Hamilton said. "Those infernal contraptions are what gave Freedonia the advantage in the Reunion War. Those goddamned things cost me a lot of money in property damage!"

"You better get on over beneath that outcropping of rock," Caleb said, nodding toward the mountains. "Me and my army will handle this."

Hamilton stared at him.

“What?” Caleb said.

Hamilton said, flatly, “If you attack that Dragonfly, the Freedonia Border Guards will see it and call it in. More Dragonflies will come and we will all die.”

Caleb opened his mouth to protest and then closed it. “Fine,” he said. “We’ll keep it cool and quiet for now. So, what's the plan?”

“We can’t even hope he hasn’t seen the pillars of dust this house throws up. He has spotted us all right.

“He’ll make three passes,” Eliza chimed in. “The first one high, as an initial check. The second time, he will come in low just to make sure. The third pass, he will call in a company of Light Infantry to check us out and demand our explanation for being here.”

The Dragonfly continued its approach, high but nearer now.

“So,” Caleb began, “we either get him the second pass he makes, or we’re caught anyway.”

“Not if we’re smart,” Hamilton said. “And that, I am. I also possess the gift of gab. I will talk our way into Freedonia. They will insist on inspecting the house, however.”

“So, what do we do, then?” Caleb asked.

“*We* do nothing,” Hamilton replied. “*You* and your army are going to sneak out through the trap door in the basement and then you are on your own.”

“Hold up a minute, Hamilton,” Caleb protested.

“I haven’t got time to argue with you,” Hamilton said. “Go now, before it is too late.”

“Damn it!” Caleb spat. “Okay.”

Caleb headed for the door.

“Good luck,” Hamilton said. “Oh, and sorry you didn’t get the opportunity to kill me and my wife and take the Ann Eliza Jane as your palace.”

Caleb looked as if he had been struck by lightning.

Hamilton laughed. “Oh, the walls have ears.”

“Oh, we’ll meet again soon, boy,” Caleb said with a smile. “That, I guarantee.”

Caleb left the room, slamming the door behind him.

The Dragonfly roared in on its first pass.

The cyclogyro stopped in mid air a few yards past the house, hovered, turned and then came back.

"Here he comes," Eliza said.

Something crashed into the underside of the Dragonfly. A moment later, a loud boom, accompanied by a flash of fire, erupted from the aircraft.

The Dragonfly wobbled and shuddered and then it burst into a black and orange cloud of fire and smoke.

"Caleb!" Hamilton roared. "God damn that monster!"

Hamilton watched in horror as scores of Freedonian soldiers sprinted toward the house. They would call for Hamilton's surrender and if he did not do so immediately, they would call in a fleet of Dragonflies and not even the *Ann Eliza Jane* could withstand that."

Caleb and his army came out of hiding from behind rocks and high grass and then plowed toward the Freedonian soldiers.

Hamilton placed a firm hand on Eliza's shoulder. "Take us out of here while both sides are distracted. Hopefully, they will all kill each other."

"Back to New York?" Eliza inquired.

"No," Hamilton said. "We park the *Ann Eliza Jane* in Richmond."

"And then?" Eliza said.

Hamilton pointed straight ahead out of the observation window. "And then, onward, to Atlanta."

CHAPTER TWENTY-TWO

September 28, 1870

The Grasshopper landed on West Paces Road, about a mile from the National House.

Harriet and Mary waited for the blades of the immense cyclogyro to stop spinning and then they hopped out onto the road.

Harriet walked toward Peachtree Road. Mary continued up West Paces.

"The National House is this way," Harriet said.

"I know," Mary said. "I can smell Douglass'

cologne. Know what I smell this way, though?"

Harriet raised an eyebrow. "What?"

"Beer and whiskey and cigars and pine oil," Mary replied. "The scents of paradise!"

"Hell is comin' and you goin' to a saloon?" Harriet said, pursing her lips.

Mary shrugged. "What better place to be when Hell comes?"

"Whatever," Harriet said. "Meet me at the National House in an hour. We gotta strategize on how to stop Caleb. I'm surprised he ain't made it here yet."

"I ain't picked up no scent of ghuls yet," Mary said. "I'll see you soon, though."

Harriet threw up her hand and jogged off.

****

Harriet entered President Douglass' office. The President sat at his desk, sipping tea. Sitting across from him was a man Harriet didn't recognize. The man's smile was warm enough, but his eyes were as cold as the grave.

"Madame Vice President! Welcome," President Douglass said, rising from his chair.

"Mr. President," Harriet replied.

The man with the warm smile and cold eyes extended his hand toward Harriet. "Madame Vice President, so nice to meet you. My name is Jeremiah G. Hamilton and I have come to help make Freedonia the wealthiest nation in the world."

Harriet shook Hamilton's hand. The world tilted and a blanket of hot, moist darkness engulfed her.

****

Mary sat at the bar of the *Gaston Saloon* taking gulps of whiskey from a half full decanter between puffs from her cigar.

The owner and bartender, Keith Gaston, exchanged limericks to the amusement of the five other patrons.

"There was a young belle of old Natchez," Mary crooned. "Whose garments were always in patchez. When comments arose on the state of her clothes, she replied, *'When Ah itchez, Ah scratchez.'*"

"Bully!" the bartender said. "Here's one for ya': A wonderful bird is the pelican; his beak can hold more than his belican. He can hold in his beak enough food for a week, though I'm damned if I know how the helican!"

Mary laughed. She took a sip of whiskey and then slapped the bar top with her palm. The bar shook. "Damn good one, Keith! I can top that, though: A flea and a fly in a flue were imprisoned, so what could they do? Said the fly, 'let us flee!' 'Let us fly!' said the flea. So they flew through a flaw in the flue."

The bar erupted in laughter and applause.

"Ah, we're being clever, are we?" Gaston said. "Ok, well, here is one I picked up from none other than Dr. George Washington Carver himself: There was a young lady named Bright, who traveled much faster than light. She set out one day in a relative way, and came back the previous night."

The patrons in the bar paused, letting the word play sink in. All at once, it seemed, they got it and they laughed.

Mary stared at the bartender for a long while. Then she spoke: "There was an old man with a beard; a funny old man with a beard. He had a big beard; a great big old beard; that amusing old man with a beard."

The patrons laughed.

Keith Gaston bowed. With that, I concede. You are truly the Goddess of wordplay!"

Mary curtsied. “You just tellin’ me what I been known, Keith. ‘Bout time somebody recognized, though. To celebrate this victory...the next round is on me!”

A cheer rose from the bar.

****

Harriet crept up Broadway in Manhattan, straining to see through the thick cloud of brown smoke. The cloud reeked of burnt sugar, kudzu and feces.

The ground shook violently, rending a massive, jagged wound in the earth. A great dragon burst forth out of the chasm, rising skyward. The dragon descended, breathing fire that scorched the tall buildings and the ground.

Harriet saw its face. It was Hamilton’s face and Caleb’s face all at once – a twisted visage of darkness, betrayal and death. The dragon’s crimson and azure body was composed of ghuls that writhed and roared in a discordant mess.

Harriet fired the Carver Mule, striking the dragon in its left eye.

The dragon roared with a thousand agonized voices. It opened its mouth wide and sped toward Harriet.

The world tilted again.

****

It was Rosetta Douglass who first saw the specks in the sky. She had been out on the lawn of the National House, pretending to tend to the beautiful white roses she planted there over a year ago. In actuality, she was visiting with Lieutenant Clarence Smith, a Freedonian officer and Honor Guard with who she was madly in love. She had looked up into Lieutenant Smith's eyes when she saw them high in the sky, over his head – specks with tails of fire.

Her outcry brought her mother, Anna and President Douglass after her onto the lawn, where they became stone effigies with pounding hearts, screening their eyes with their hands as they stared skyward. The specks appeared in view of a landscape that centuries of civilization had fertilized and cultivated and formed.

Beyond the National House loomed Friendship A.M.E. Church. Rosetta always referred to Friendship A.M.E. as 'Friend'. She had a habit of personifying all inanimate things; a habit that began in childhood and continued beyond her recent 30th birthday. If the Friendship A.M.E. walls were covered with hoarfrost, she said that her *friend* was shivering; if the wind tore around the church's tower, she said that her *friend* had gas from overindulging in her mother's corned beef hash.

A century older than the specks in the sky was Rosetta's *friend*; but the pass road was many more, countless more, centuries older than any *friend* of Rosetta's. It had been a trail for Native American tribes long before any white man claimed to have discovered it and then claimed it as his own. Rosetta saw how the legions of fawn, light yellow-brown, sinewy men, covered in crimson, looked in their close ranks as they soared across the noonday sky.

Many wars had passed the church and many more had passed the land upon which the church sat. Stone axe, spear and bow, javelin and broadsword, blunderbuss and steam-powered cannon – all the weapons, of all stages in the art of war – had gone trooping past. Now had come the specks in the sky, like a swarm of alien wasps pouring out of a tear in the Lumineferous Aether.

****

Mary sniffed the air.

"Excuse me," Keith Gaston said. "My wife made me two fried eggs this morning with a side of pinto beans."

"That smells pretty bad," Mary said. "But what I'm smellin' is a lot worse. You should go home to your wife, now."

"What?" The bartender said. "We don't close until around ten o'clock; sometimes a little later. We have another ten or eleven hours to go."

"Naw," Mary said. "You about to close – or *be* closed – right now!"

"Now, wait just a minute," Gaston snapped. "I..."

Mary dove behind the bar's counter, pulling the bartender down with her, just before a squad of ghuls burst into the bar and opened fire. Bullets flew over their heads. Bottles shattered, raining rum, gin and whiskey on them.

"Waste not; want not," Mary said, grabbing a glass and then using it to catch samples of the different spirits. She emptied the glass in one gulp.

When the volley of bullets stopped, Mary focused her hearing. The men were reloading. She peeked out from under the counter. There were a dozen gunmen; well, not really *men* anymore; there were a dozen gun*ghuls*.

Mary drew both Dragoon revolvers and fired a volley of her own. The ghuls dove for cover.

She wounded several and delivered fatal hits to three of them – one in the chest; one in the upper spine and one right between the eyes.

Mary barely had enough time to duck again before more bullets flew past her.

She raised her carbine over the counter and, using the ghuls' heartbeats as guides, fired off several rounds at an overturned table she had seen a few of the ghuls take cover behind. The bullets pierced the tables, finding their marks on the other side.

Three ghuls fell from behind the table, collapsing in bloody heaps on the hardwood floor.

Another hail of lead crashed into the reinforced bar. One of them grazed Mary's leg, another hit her arm.

The bullets ricocheted off of Mary's stone-hard flesh. One lodged in the wall beside Mary. The other bullet tore a hole in the bartender's head.

Mary slid over the alcohol-wet floor to the leftmost edge of the bar, away from the gunfire, reloading as she glided along.

She popped up onto one knee and then returned fire.

More ghuls fell.

She rose, unloading her rifle and twin pistols.

Ghuls fell like a torrential rain of fetid flesh and greenish-black blood.

****

Harriet's eyes flew open. Wide-eyed, she examined her surroundings. She was still in President Douglass' office, alone. Someone – probably Douglass – had laid her on the President's couch.

She had to warn him. That man, Hamilton, was responsible for the Great Fire in Manhattan – probably in her world and in this one – and was in cahoots with Caleb Butler.

She stood and then walked to the arched French windows at the back of the office. She looked out onto the lawn. Scattered about were the corpses of Freedonian soldiers and Hwarang ghuls.

"Lawd, have mercy!" Harriet said. "Lawd, why you send me that message with Caleb and his army so close? I hope Mary is out there handling this."

Harriet whirled on her heels and dashed out of the office.

****

Mary tiptoed out of the saloon. She focused her vision. About a mile away, nearly a hundred ghuls charged up West Paces Road, murdering all within their view.

She focused her hearing. Screams of fear and agony assaulted her ears.

"Damn!" She sighed.

Mary drew a brass Very pistol from a pocket inside of her waistcoat. She pointed the gun toward the sky and pulled the trigger. A glowing, bright red flare rocketed high into the air. She then ran to a parked steam car, dropped into a prone position and then shimmied under the vehicle.

A few minutes later, a Grasshopper cyclogyro, piloted by Major Clark, landed a few yards away from where Mary fired the flare.

Mary crawled from under the car and sprang to her feet. She focused her vision again. The ghuls were a quarter of a mile away, now. She sprinted toward the Grasshopper and leapt into it.

"I hope you summoned me for a lift to the National House" Major Clark said. "Those monsters are killing us out there."

“Naw,” Mary said. “But I think I got somethin’ for those damned ghuls.”

“Ghuls...so that’s what you call them,” Colonel Clark said.

“Yep,” Mary replied.

“Where to, then?” Major Clark asked.

Mary pointed toward the North. “The Tuskegee Institute.”

****

Sounds of war filled the air. Metal rang against metal, and the unearthly cries of the inhuman ghuls unnerved the normally steely Freedonian soldiers.

Into the fray Harriet went, releasing the power of her spirit, and crushing as many of the Hwarang that swarmed the National House as she could.

She struck at the ghuls with frightening speed, ferocity and violence, forcing them back, casting them high into the air, driving them into the hard soil until their bones cracked and their flesh was torn asunder.

She cut a path of blood and broken bodies through the battle.

Harriet pushed through another dense line of Freedonian soldiers who were trading blows with Hwarang and other ghuls. She climbed a low hill where the Ghul King and his Council stood looking north and west. She was exhausted, yet she summoned strength from a reserve and pushed through the waves of ghul sailors and Hwarang who protected their king.

In the distance, she saw dark lines of more ghuls marching toward her.

Harriet shot again and again, until her fingers were raw flesh. She paused for a moment, allowing them to heal and then fired another volley from the *Carver Mule.*

A score of ghuls fell dead.

She charged the Hwarang ghuls, colliding with a crack of iron and wood. She slashed with her spadroon and felt the impact of bone snap against the blade. She felt the weight of Freedonian soldiers pushing in from the front as well as at her back, curses and screams and iron raking against iron and the rending of flesh.

Harriet felt the riptide of ghuls falter as the fighting shifted to the left. She saw a break in the line and lunged forward, stabbing to her left with the point of her sword.

The steel tip ripped into flesh and bone.

A Hwarang ghul fell to the ground at Harriet's feet.

She stepped over the fallen body, attacking the next creature who tried to fill the gap. She stabbed the ghul in the throat.

The Hwarang ghul's blood sprayed – a fine mist, warm and red-green. The monster grabbed at the sword stuck in his neck.

Harriet ripped the sword free. Another gush of blood.

The ghul grasped at the wound as he fell to his knees choking and gurgling on his own ichor.

"Naleul ssaum , manyeo!" – *"Fight me, witch!"* – Colonel Kim howled.

Harriet snapped her head toward the direction of the voice. The Hwarang Colonel charged toward her, sword at the ready.

Harriet pushed through the crowd of battling Freedonians and ghuls, her sword held above her head. She stood at an opening a few yards from the melee, whirling her spadroon before her.

"Isanghan... na-ege manyeo leul hochul goemul," Harriet said. *"Funny...a monster calling me a witch."*

"Dangsin-eun Hangug-eoleul!" – "You speak the language of Joseon," Colonel Kim said. "Where did you learn?"

"Here and there," Harriet replied.

"Well, in war, we are all monsters, are we not?" Colonel Kim said.

"Some, more than others," Harriet said.

Colonel Kim nodded. "Indeed."

Tightening her grip on her sword, Harriet approached Colonel Kim. As she closed, Colonel Kim fell into an easy stance, geom sword raised behind his head. Harriet adjusted her step, circling to her right — just outside the reach of Colonel Kim's sword swing.

The Colonel shuffled, shifting to keep Harriet in front of him. He held himself with an easy confidence, assured in the superiority of his two-handed long sword and the brigandine armor vest and greaves he wore under his garments. His reach was longer; he had no reason to attack first. Harriet would have to get in closer to use her spadroon, and during that time, Colonel Kim would have a chance to use the geom.

"Arrogance is good," Harriet thought. *"Pride always cometh before a fall."*

She continued to drift around the Hwarang ghul leader, maintaining the same distance and letting the tip of her sword dance hypnotically before him while her mind unconsciously focused on the subtle changes in Colonel Kim's posture and position.

The sun beat down, and Harriet felt sweat bead up on her neck and drip down the inside of her arms within her blouse.

Having completed two complete circuits of the Colonel's stationary position, Harriet settled into a low stance, sword ready, and waited.

She did not have to wait long.

The Colonel leapt forward, the geom lashing out at Harriet's neck. It was a marvelously delivered blow, but for all the swiftness of Colonel Kim's attack, signs of his intent had been readily clear to Harriet.

As the geom snapped toward her, Harriet stepped forward and to the outside, slamming the pommel of her sword and her left forearm against the Colonel's arm, blocking the blow before it could even be fully extended.

Colonel Kim reacted quickly, folding his arm back and bending it at the elbow. His momentum carried him forward, and his elbow hit Harriet hard at the base of her rib cage.

Harriet felt half her breath abandon her body. She tightened her abdomen to retain enough air in her lungs to fight on.

She felt the sword coming. As the geom came hurtling down, Harriet darted to her left.

As she moved, she raised her sword. The blade slashed across the Colonel's throat.

Metal rang off metal with no sign of blood. His armored shirt had saved him from the fatal cut.

Colonel Kim countered with a slash of his own.

Harriet took a slight step backward with her lead leg.

The geom blade whirled past her nose.

Harriet thrust her sword up into Colonel Kim's left armpit, exposed after his failed attack.

The Colonel collapsed around Harriet's spadroon, grunting in pain.

Harriet grabbed the shoulder of Colonel Kim's robe, clutching a fistful of cloth. She pulled the cloth toward her chest, yanking Colonel Kim off balance. It would be easy to throw him now. Once the Colonel was on the ground, the protection provided by his armor would be negated and it would be much easier to deliver a finishing attack.

Fire exploded across Harriet's back.

Colonel Kim had managed to twist the geom and plant it into Harriet's back, just missing her spine.

Struggling through the pain, Harriet drove her right knee into Colonel Kim's groin.

Colonel Kim staggered backward.

Harriet's back muscles shrieked in agony as Colonel Kim tried to hang on to the geom as he stumbled.

Harriet managed to twist away and pull the handle from the Colonel's fingers. She reached behind her, desperately trying to grasp the haft of the geom lodged in her flesh. More pain lanced up her back and into the base of her skull as she twisted her body. Her fingers slipped on the bloody handle.

Colonel Kim wobbled, his legs struggling to hold him upright. Harriet caught sight of a shadow at the base of his neck. Her spadroon had cut the Hwarang leader after all. Not fatally, but she had drawn blood.

Harriet's hand found the haft of the geom and pulled it free. Now she had two swords.

Colonel Kim exploded forward, raising his straight leg high until his knee touched his chest. He then whipped his leg in a downward arc toward the top of Harriet's head.

Harriet darted to her left, sweeping the bloody geom up and slamming its handle against the bones in Colonel Kim's ankle.

The Colonel cried out in agony. In desperation, he snapped his right hand out, driving his metal-shod fist into Harriet's throat.

Harriet's throat closed. Gagging, she felt her grip on the geom loosen. The Colonel struck again.

Harriet barely managed to tuck her chin down.

Colonel Kim's fist scraped across her jaw.

Harriet stumbled backward.

Colonel Kim pressed his advantage, pounding Harriet with short jabs.

Harriet reeled from the blows. Blood poured from her nose.

Colonel Kim coiled his back and then launched a powerful palm strike toward Harriet's solar plexus.

Harriet jabbed upward with Colonel Kim's geom, shoving the point of the blade into the base of the Hwarang's hand.

Colonel Kim's fingers closed into a fist. His wrist cocked at a strange angle.

Harriet felt the knife grind against bone. She shoved and twisted the blade.

The Colonel screamed.

Harriet dropped her hips and twisted her body around as she swept her right leg backward.

Colonel Kim flew off his feet.

Harriet, still holding onto his arm, fell with him. They crashed to the ground. A bone-snapping crunch followed.

Harriet rolled to her feet.

The leader of the Hwarang struggled to turn over. His right arm flopped lifelessly against his side – the hand had been run-through by Harriet's sword, and the elbow was bent at a hideous angle. The sleeve of the Colonel's white robe was now dyed burgundy by blood.

The Colonel Kim flopped onto his back, screaming and crying.

Harriet knelt beside the downed Colonel Kim. She shoved her spadroon into his eye.

The Colonel thrashed for a moment and then his limbs stilled.

Harriet drew the *Carver Mule* from its pouch and fired in Caleb's direction.

The bullet hit Colin in the torso.

Blood splattered Caleb's chest.

Colin collapsed. A line of smoke rose from a gaping hole in Colin's back.

Connor dropped to his knees beside his brother. "Colin! No!"

Harriet fired again.

Connor's head disappeared. His headless frame fell over on its side.

"Rip her apart!" Caleb commanded.

Hordes of ghuls rushed her from all sides.

Harriet fired volley after volley with the *Carver Mule* as she slashed, stabbed and hacked away with her sword.

Many ghuls fell. Many more took their place.

The ghuls overwhelmed Harriet,

pummeling her and clawing her flesh.

"I guess it's my time, Lawd," Harriet whispered. "I'll see you directly."

Harriet heard a loud buzzing overhead. A moment later, the ghuls skittered away from her and rallied around Caleb.

The Ghul King and his subjects were covered in a pinkish-green goo; the same pinkish-green goo from Dr. Carver's laboratory – the Carver Mushroom.

Harriet looked up toward the buzzing. A Grasshopper flew overhead. The door to the Grasshopper opened and Mary leapt out. She landed on the ground with a thunderous din.

"Happy you decided to join us, Mary, Harriet said. "*After* I was almost killed."

"The key word is *almost*," Mary said.

"What have you done?" Caleb hissed. "What is this?"

"*That* is the Carver Mushroom," Mary said, drawing one of her revolvers. "Your end. Mine, too."

Mary jammed the muzzle of the gun into the soft tissue behind her chin.

“Mary!” Harriet gasped. “What are you doing?”

“Yeah, negress,” Caleb said. “What are you…errk…King Louis was the King of France before the revolution; and then he got his head cut off, which spoiled his constitution… annyeonghaseyo… annyeonghi jumusyeoss-eoyo.”

The ghuls repeated the nonsensical chattering of their King.

“See, Harriet,” Mary said. “The mushrooms are connecting all of our consciousnesses. I feel its pull, too. We are becoming one.”

“So?” Harriet said.

“So, if one of us dies, we all die.” Mary said.

“Mary, don’t do this,” Harriet said. A tear fell from the corner of Harriet’s eye.

“I’m already dead, Harriet,” Mary said. “How long do you think the MAHO can contain my power? I’ll burn out in months. And if I don’t do this, the world will be overrun by Caleb and his army within a fortnight.”

Harriet reached for Mary’s gun. “Mary!”

Mary backpedaled away from Harriet. "I've already infected the ghuls at the National House and the ones on West Paces."

"Mary, please," Harriet cried.

"It's the only way," Mary said.

"I know," Harriet replied.

"I love you, sis," Mary sobbed.

Harriet turned away from Mary and walked away. "I love you, too, Mary."

A shot echoed across the sky.

Ghuls collapsed all around Harriet, for as far as her eyes could see.

She peered over her shoulder. Stagecoach Mary lay, face down on the ground. Caleb lay dead a few yards away from her. The surviving Freedonian soldiers struggled to their feet and then busied themselves tended to their wounded and to their dead.

"Lawd," Harriet sighed as she walked away. It was time for her to heal and to mourn the loss of a dear friend before heading home.

CHAPTER TWENTY-THREE

October 1, 1870

Harriet and Dr. Carver walked into Friendship A.M.E. Church. The church was empty. Most churches were at three a.m. Harriet followed Dr. Carver to the pulpit. Dr. Carver placed the palms of his hands on the floor. A panel beneath Dr. Carver's hands opened, revealing a ladder descending into darkness. Dr. Carver descended the ladder. Harriet followed suit.

At the bottom of the ladder was a small room. Within that small room was a single item: the Spirit Engine.

"Here we are," Dr. Carver said. "Thank you, for all that you have done."

"You're welcome," Harriet said. "This has been an interesting journey and I am happy I could help."

"I thought I was stronger than a word," Dr. Carver said. "But I just discovered that having to say goodbye to you is by far the hardest thing I've ever had to do, Harriet."

"Don't be silly," Harriet said. "You *still* have a Harriet Tubman."

"She is very much not you," Dr. Carver said. And as you said, I will see her again soon, but I wonder how you say goodbye to someone forever?"

"I reckon you just say 'goodbye," Harriet replied.

"Well, goodbye, Moses," Dr. Carver said.

"Goodbye Dr. Carver."

Dr. Carver pulled the lever on the Spirit Engine. A moment later, a tear opened before Harriet. She leapt through it. The tear closed and then it – and Harriet – vanished.

CHAPTER TWENTY-FOUR

January 1, 1871

The members of Mount Gilboa Chapel filed out of the tiny church eating bowls of Hoppin' John – a dish of black-eyed peas and rice eaten on New Year's Day to bring a prosperous year filled with good luck – and collard greens for wealth and prosperity.

Below the church, Banneker laughed at the superstition as he sipped tea from a straw. The tea – steeped in a pot attached to his gurney was his favorite, Tieguanyin – named after the Buddhist deity, Guan Yin, the Iron Goddess of

Mercy – the most expensive tea in the world, revered for its chestnut flavor, golden color and, most of all, for the distinct, pitch perfect ringing sound it made when poured into a cup.

Familiar footsteps approached.

"Ah, I see you were successful in your separation," Banneker said.

"Yeah," Caleb said, stepping close enough for Banneker to see him. "But you forgot to mention that damned Jek creature was guardin' the Spirit-Engine and that's how me and John Brown would wind up separated."

"I honestly thought that was merely a rumor concocted by Baas Bello to scare away potential seekers of the device," Banneker said. "I thought the journey to the parallel reality would tear you apart."

"Oh, it did," Caleb said. "If Brown had made it over to that other reality, he wouldn't have survived nohow. It was my...fluidity that allowed me to survive."

"I trust Baas Bello is dead," Banneker said.

"If he wasn't would I be here?" Caleb asked.

"True," Banneker replied. "But wait...how

did you return to our reality?"

The corners of Caleb's mouth stretched across his cheeks in an impossibly wide grin. "Through your mama's knickers."

"What?!" Banneker bellowed.

Caleb laughed so hard his shoulders shook. His laughter grew louder; the shaking of his shoulders more violent.

"Caleb…Mr. Butler…what is the meaning of this?" Banneker inquired.

Caleb answered with more laughter. His entire body shook now, so violently that large chunks of flesh sloughed off and fell, in a sticky pile, at his feet.

"What in the hell!" Banneker shouted.

Caleb's laughter grew more rapid, becoming a cackle that scratched at Banneker's few living nerve endings. The Ghul King's face fell from his skull, sliding down the front of his shirt until it plopped onto the top of the flesh pile.

"No!" Banneker screamed.

The laughter stopped.

Caleb was gone. Standing before Banneker

was Harriet. She raised the *Bello Mule* and fired, hitting Banneker in the chest.

Banneker screamed in agony.

"I am immortal, woman," he coughed. "So, save your bullets."

"I know I can't kill you, Banneker," Harriet said. "But there's worse things than death."

"You think I don't know that?" Banneker hissed. "I am trapped in this useless body for eternity – a body made useless by your lover! All I have left is my sharp and brilliant mind."

"And you won't have that for much longer," Harriet said.

Banneker laughed. "Fool, you can barely read; you have no chance of breaking a mind such as this."

"I beg to differ," Harriet said, with a snap of her fingers.

The second illusion faded. Banneker was no longer in the bowels of Mount Gilboa Chapel. He now rested in a hole in the earth.

"W-where am I?" Banneker croaked. "Harriet, what have you done?"

"I've hurt you, and I'm gon' go on hurtin'

you...forever."

Harriet grabbed a shovel that rested in a mound of dirt beside her. She scooped up a pile of dirt and then poured it into the hole. Chunks of soft red dirt rained upon Banneker's mask.

"There is no red dirt in Oella, or in all of Maryland," Banneker said. "Where have you taken me?"

"Oh, here and there," Harriet said, scooping more dirt into the hole.

"How? My knolls..."

"Are destroyed," Harriet chimed in. "Your lab and all your life's work, too."

Harriet shoveled another scoop of dirt into the hole, covering Banneker's dead legs.

"As far as how you wound up here...your faithful, poor, feeble-minded Mary Elizabeth Bowser ain't at all poor or feeble-minded and damn sure ain't faithful to no monster like you. She was happy to slip a little somethin' in yo' drink that made sho' you slept like a baby until I was ready for you to wake up."

"Mary Elizabeth?" Banneker sobbed. "No!

"Yep," Harriet chuckled.

More red dirt fell into the hole.

"Harriet...please," Banneker cried. "I will give you riches beyond your wildest imagination."

"You ain't listenin'," Harriet said. "We destroyed everything of yours. Your story ends here. You put a period on it the minute you sent Caleb and John Brown after Baas. They dead, too, by the way."

"So, Baas Bello has finally won and he is not here to gloat and to celebrate his victory?"

"You weren't worth his time," Harriet replied. "He had mo' important matters to attend to...getting' his toenails clipped I think it was."

"Harriet! No!" Banneker wailed.

The scrape of the shovel and the tumble of cold dirt soon muffled his pleas.

Harriet patted the loose soil over Banneker's grave and then hurled the shovel off into the dense forest that surrounded her. She turned away from the mound and as she walked away, she looked skyward.

"Lawd," she began, "I know a man deserves a prayer when he's buried, but I ain't one for prayin' for my enemies. I knows you forgives me, Lawd, 'cause I keeps Heaven filled with fresh souls. I know, too, that my fightin' days is close to an end, but let my lovin' days be long, 'cause me and Baas got some catchin' up to do. Amen!"

Steamfunk, Alternate History And A Country Called Freedonia

By Milton J. Davis

The year is 1870. As the young country of Freedonia prepares to celebrate fifty years of existence, a young bounty hunter by the name of Zeke Culpepper is hired by a wealthy businessman to find a valuable book. In the kingdom of Mali on the continent of Africa, veteran warrior Famara Keita has been assigned to find that same book and bring it back to its rightful owner. And in the newly formed nation of Germany, an ambitious Prussian officer seeks the book as well for its secrets that could make

Germany the most powerful nation in the world. The result is an action adventure like no other.

--From Here to Timbuktu

I'm a history nut from way back. As a matter of fact, until I was in high school all my extra-curricular reading was History. From dinosaurs, to World War II to eventually African history, I was and I still am fascinated about things that were. I'm not dazzled by dates and names, but by the personalities, customs and cultures of the past.

Despite my love of history, I haven't been much of a fan of *alternate* history. I've read a few novels and I've been slightly interested, but my question has always been, 'where *we* at?' It seems that all the authors that write alternate history, at least the ones I've read, either completely ignore people of color or as far as they are concerned, people of African descent always end up being slaves. The only difference is the duration of internment.

So imagine my shock when I discovered Lion's Blood by Steve Barnes!

Here was an intelligent and fascinating alternate history where Africans settled North America and those who became slaves were of Irish descent. It was not a wish fulfillment book, but a thoughtful analysis of the condition of slavery and the effects on both master and slave.

When I first laid the groundwork for MVmedia, one of my ideas was an alternate history based on the questions: *What if the Haitian Revolution spread to the southeastern United States? What if, with the help from Haitian soldiers, it succeeded?* And *What if the new country of Haiti claimed French territory as its own?* The result of such musing is the maps displayed at the end of this book of the country of ***Freedonia***, a country that serves as the background of my *Steamfunk* anthology story *The Delivery*, my novel, *From Here to Timbuktu* and this novel you now hold in your hands. Freedonia is a country where in the 1870's Fredrick Douglass is president, Harriet Tubman is Vice President, George Washington Carver is the scientific genius behind Freedonia's prosperity and W.E.B. DuBois is an industrialist rivaling Getty and Rockefeller.

So this is where I'll be hanging out for a while. I hope you like where my Steamfunk is coming from. Pull up a rocking chair, have some sweet tea, and let me tell you a story.

Because It's Tastier Than Bacon And Thicker Than Three-Day Old Grits!

That's *"Why should you read the entire Chronicles of Harriet Tubman series, From Here to Timbuktu and the Steamfunk anthology?"* for a thousand dollars, Alex!

While some might argue that *nothing* is tastier than bacon – the *Chronicles of Harriet Tubman* series is certainly tastier than *turkey* bacon and, without a doubt, is thicker than three-day old grits.

Hold the series in your hands...that's it!

See?

Now, I would argue that the *Chronicles of Harriet Tubman* series is much tastier than bacon. Whether you agree or not, however, you *must* agree that the *Chronicles of Harriet*

Tubman series and bacon share some uncanny similarities.

Let's explore the worldwide love affair with bacon and how it is indicative of the success of the *Chronicles of Harriet Tubman* series:

Why do we love bacon?

According to a recent scientific study, it is due to the *Maillard Reaction,* a form of nonenzymatic browning, which results from a chemical reaction between an amino acid and a reducing sugar. This reaction produces a wide range of molecules that vary in flavor and smell and is what gives us the flavor of toasted bread, roasted coffee, chocolate, caramel and – of course – bacon.

Bacon is made of mostly protein, water and fat. The protein is made up of the building blocks we call amino acids. The fat contains reducing sugars. Get that bacon really hot and the Maillard Reaction starts. And the smell of that sizzling bacon is enough to tempt even the staunchest of vegetarians.

And somehow you know, dear vegetarians...there is something deeper going on inside that sizzling meat. There's some complex chemistry going on.

Well, the funky goodness that is the *Chronicles of Harriet Tubman* series occurs just like that bacon.

Scientists refer to the phenomenon as the *Ojetade Reaction*, a form of creativity and determination born out of a desire to see great Steamfunk stories – Steampunk told from an Afrikan and Afrikan-Diasporan perspective.

After a conversation with other authors online, in which we decided to tell our stories in this fascinating subgenre of science fiction and fantasy called Steampunk and to call such stories Steamfunk, Milton Davis decided to produce an anthology of Steamfunk stories. I came to Milton and offered my services as Co-Editor, extolling my knowledge of Steampunk, my Steamfunk / Steampunk blog and my bestselling Steamfunk book, *Moses: The Chronicles of Harriet Tubman*. After about five minutes of contemplation, Milton sighed *"Okay, you can be Co-Editor,"* and followed this with a barely whispered *"Damn!"*

I think that *"Damn!"* Was Milton's way of saying *"Oh, happy day,"* or something to that effect.

We then posted a call for submissions and received a surprising twenty-one – we didn't know so many people were interested in telling

Steamfunk stories. While all of the stories were incredible, we picked the twelve most funktastic ones and Milton and this author added a story each to this Blacknificent mix.

Marcellus Shane Jackson created some hot artwork and voila...the *Steamfunk* anthology was born.

The funk created by this thrilling anthology was enough to spark other great works of Steamfunk you should pick up: *Mona Livelong: Paranormal Detective* by Valjeanne Jeffers and *From Here to Timbuktu* by Milton Davis. This final (?) installment of the *Chronicles of Harriet Tubman* series – along with *From Here to Timbuktu* – is set in Milton Davis' alternate world of Freedonia.

Wild, huh?

Yep. And *tasty*. So, dive into some great Steamfunk and devour it all.

You can thank me the next time you run into me at a Con, or on the street, in the airport, in a Thai restaurant anywhere in the world, or on a cruise ship to Hawaii – my usual stomping grounds. Just not at an Anthony Hamilton concert. That would just be creepy.

ABOUT THE AUTHOR

Afrikan Martial Arts Master and Babalawo / Olorisa / Elegbe, Balogun is the author of the bestselling non-fiction books *Afrikan Martial Arts: Discovering the Warrior Within*, *The Afrikan Warriors Bible* and *The Young Afrikan Warriors' Guide to Defeating Bullies & Trolls.* He is screenwriter / producer / director of the films, *A Single Link*, *Rite of Passage: Initiation* and *Rite of Passage: The Dentist of Westminster.*

Balogun is one of the leading authorities on Steamfunk – a philosophy or style of writing that combines the African and / or African American culture and approach to life with that of the steampunk philosophy and / or steampunk fiction – and writes about it, the craft of writing, Sword & Soul and Steampunk in general, at http://chroniclesofharriet.com/.

He is author of nine novels – the Steamfunk

bestseller, *MOSES: The Chronicles of Harriet Tubman (Books 1 & 2)*; the Urban Science Fiction saga, *Redeemer*; the Sword & Soul epic, *Once Upon A Time In Afrika*; a Fight Fiction, New Pulp novella, *Fist of Afrika*; the gritty, Urban Superhero series, *A Single Link* and *Wrath of the Siafu*; the two-fisted Dieselfunk tale, *The Scythe*, the "Choose-Your-Own-Destiny"-style Young Adult novel, *The Keys* and the Urban Fantasy epic, *Redeemer: The Cross Chronicles*. Balogun is also contributing co-editor of two anthologies: *Ki: Khanga: The Anthology* and *Steamfunk*.

Finally, Balogun is the Director and Fight Choreographer of the Steamfunk feature film, *Rite of Passage*, which he wrote based on the short story, *Rite of Passage*, by author Milton Davis and co-author of the award winning screenplay, *Ngolo*.

You can reach him on Facebook at www.facebook.com/Afrikan.Martial.Arts; on Twitter at https://twitter.com/Baba_Balogun and on Tumblr at www.tumblr.com/blog/blackspeculativefiction.

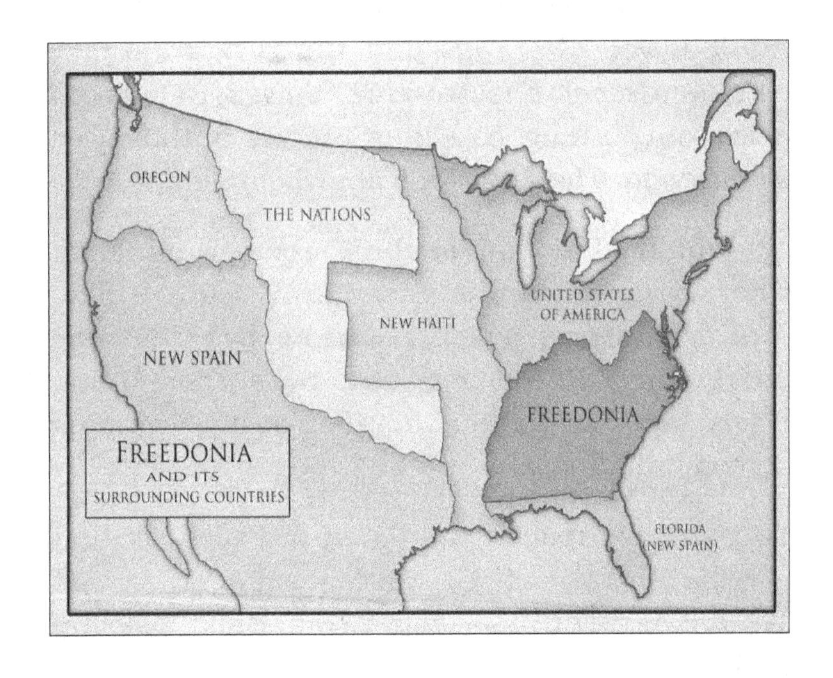
OREGON
THE NATIONS
NEW HAITI
UNITED STATES
OF AMERICA
NEW SPAIN
FREEDONIA
FREEDONIA
AND ITS
SURROUNDING COUNTRIES
FLORIDA
(NEW SPAIN)

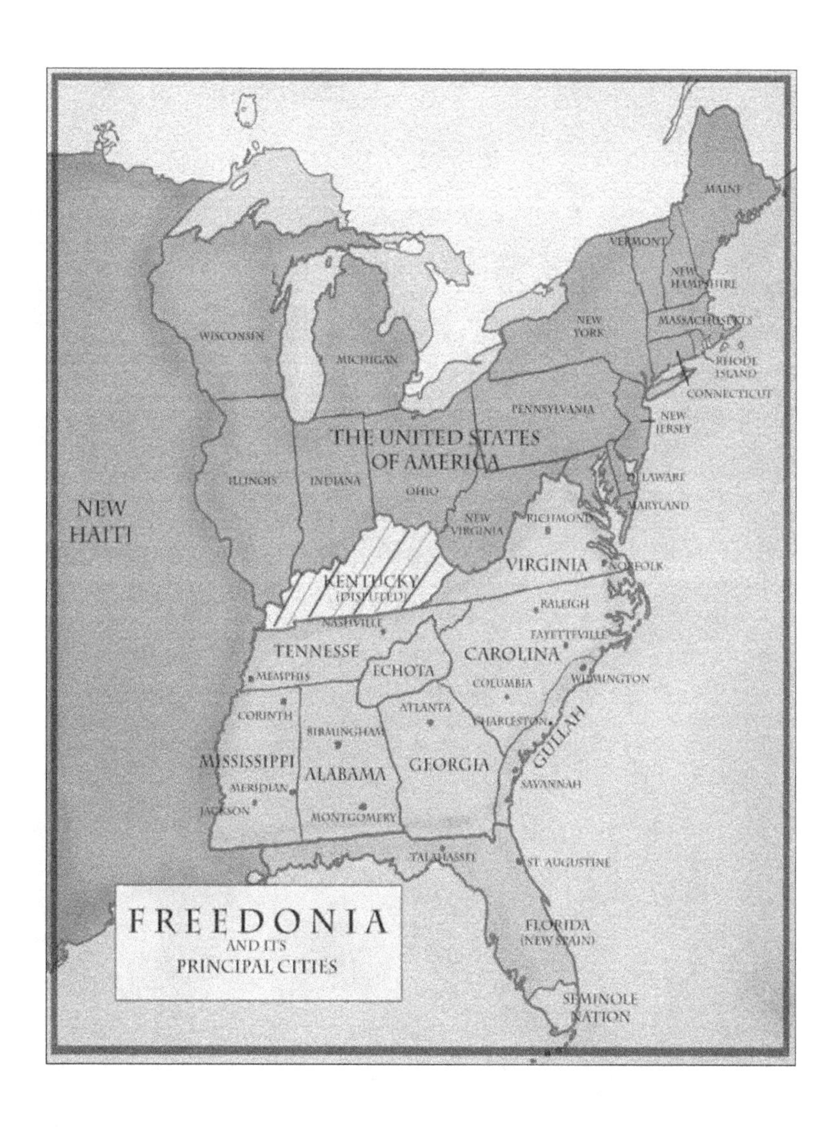
FREEDONIA
AND ITS
PRINCIPAL CITIES
THE UNITED STATES
OF AMERICA
NEW
HAITI
MAINE
VERMONT
NEW
HAMPSHIRE
MASSACHUSETTS
RHODE
ISLAND
CONNECTICUT
NEW
YORK
PENNSYLVANIA
NEW
JERSEY
DELAWARE
MARYLAND
WISCONSIN
MICHIGAN
ILLINOIS
INDIANA
OHIO
NEW
VIRGINIA
RICHMOND
VIRGINIA
NORFOLK
KENTUCKY
(DISPUTED)
NASHVILLE
TENNESSE
MEMPHIS
ECHOTA
CAROLINA
RALEIGH
FAYETTEVILLE
COLUMBIA
WILMINGTON
CHARLESTON
GULLAH
ATLANTA
CORINTH
BIRMINGHAM
MISSISSIPPI
ALABAMA
GEORGIA
MERIDIAN
JACKSON
MONTGOMERY
SAVANNAH
TALAHASSE
ST. AUGUSTINE
FLORIDA
(NEW SPAIN)
SEMINOLE
NATION

FREEDONIA
HONOR & GRACE

CPSIA information can be obtained
at www.ICGtesting.com
Printed in the USA
LVHW091326071019
633420LV00001B/201/P